Morituri

By the Author

In the Name of God

Wolf Dreams

Yasmina Khadra
MORITURI

TRANSLATED BY
David Herman

The Toby Press

First English language Edition 2003

The Toby Press LLC
POB 8531, New Milford, CT. 06676-8531, USA
& POB 2455, London WIA 5WY, England
www.tobypress.com

ISBN 1 59264 035 4, *paperback original*

A CIP catalogue record for this title
is available from the British Library

Typeset in Garamond by Jerusalem Typesetting

Printed and bound in the United States by
Thomson-Shore Inc., Michigan

The Toby Crime Series

Introduction

 As Georges Simenon once remarked, all of us, brought to extremity by a sudden change in circumstance, can be compelled into a situation in which crime seems the only possible way out. Crime novels, then, are about such extremes of human behavior and they exist in all literatures. The French call them *noirs*; in Italy they are *gialli*; we used to call them "detective stories" or "mysteries", and most English and American ones have centered on the "puzzle" or "low life" aspect. But what has brought many remarkable novelists (Dostoyevsky, Balzac, Wilkie Collins, Graham Greene) to the genre is, I suspect, not so much the solution of a puzzle, but the fact that extremities clarify human dilemmas and afford the writer a clear narrative to follow. For a century-and-a-half, readers everywhere have enjoyed them for those same reasons.

Whatever the type, all crime (or "espionage") novels, from Buchan through Le Carré, rest (to different degrees), on action and character, and involve suspense. Suspense derives from not knowing how something will work out—hence the "thriller" which compels readers to turn the pages. But there is a substantial difference—it is a matter of the emphasis placed on character and language—between the least of these (many of which afford pleasure) and those which engage the reader at a higher level, whose pleasures are richer and more lasting.

Toby Crime proposes a series in which crime novels from many literatures are first novels, and only then crime novels. That is, they are written for a literate public by writers who engage with language and society, and pose genuine human dilemmas. In that sense they go beyond crime to real life and real characters. The crime will not always be murder and they will come in all shapes and sizes, though the majority will be short. I like to think they would have been enjoyed by Simenon, Greene and Chandler, as by Ian Rankin, Henning Mankell and Elmore Leonard, among other contemporary masters of the genre.

KEITH BOTSFORD,
General Editor

To our deeply missed Houaria C. Chaiia

*A glossary of some of the Arabic terms used in this book
may be found at the end*

The greatest periods of our life are those in which we finally have the courage to declare that the evil we carry within us is the best part of ourselves.

—*Nietzsche*

Chapter one

Deprived of everything, the horizon gives birth by cesarean section to a day which, in the end, will not have been worth its pain. I get out of my bed, utterly devitalized by a sleep in which I was alert to the slightest tremor. Times are hard: misfortune strikes so quickly.

Mina snores within range of my displeasure, thick like a rancid paste, a tip of breast unconcernedly deployed at the edge of the sheet. Far gone the time when the most innocent of touches would arouse me sexually. That was the time when I had an orgasm close to the surface of the skin; the time when I could not dissociate pride from virility, positivism from procreation. Today my wife, my poor beast of burden, has regressed—she holds no more attraction than a trailer lying across the road, but at least she's there when I am afraid in the dark.

I slip on my suit, the uniform of a proletarian-in-spite-of-himself, gulp down a beverage with a bad aftertaste, and spend a good quarter of an hour on the lookout at my window in case a terrorist should take it into his head to bust my piggy-bank of prejudices. Apparently the road is clear. Apart from a street cleaner in the process of gathering some garbage, which will inevitably reappear there tomorrow, the street is as deserted as Paradise.

It's two hundred meters from my building to the garage where I park my car. Previously I would have covered the distance in a single stride. Today it's an expedition. Everything looks suspect to me. Every step is fraught with danger. At times I become so afraid that I consider turning back.

The night watchman is a good sort. He feels sorry for me. In his modest conception of things, he considers me as good as dead. He is even surprised to see that I seem to be surviving from day to day.

We haven't been close. Our relationship has been limited to "*Bonjour,*" or "*Bonsoir,*"—but he knew where to find me when he had a problem. When he would arrive suddenly at my home at impossible hours, with his defeated air, I would reassure him, time after time. I was the neighborhood's good cop, constantly available and disinterested; my shack, lacking the air of a confessional, received interminable cohorts of people on the margins of society, without distinction of morals or race. I was not the Prophet; nevertheless, it seemed to me, I had at my disposal a multitude of sheep, enough to supply ten revolutions. Then they began to shoot at my colleagues, and my universe all of a sudden became unpopulated. In the street they make out that they don't know me. Being close to a cop is to expose oneself excessively, particularly when he fires in all directions. No longer does anyone dare to make me a tiny sign, nor even a furtive glance: no one remembers the little services I used to render them, or the hornets' nest from which I would extract them.

In this country, where the winds blow from all directions, the weathervanes spin wildly. Henceforth I am 'the cop'. Period.

I am supposed to exhibit my status of privileged target and to shut up. This is why the night watchman greets me with mournful eyes and accompanies me to my car as if to a funeral. No more febrile bowing, no more trembling of the voice in his "Good morning, Monsieur superintendent," no more of that humility bordering on hypocrisy. My night watchman even permits himself a hint of condescension. Certainly he is nothing, but he risks nothing. In a sense he is taking his revenge on the social hierarchy.

I arrive at the station an hour late. Security precautions require this. We have been strongly advised—ordered in fact—to disguise our routines. The orderly accosts me the moment I cross the threshold of the establishment.

—The boss wants you.

—Tell him that I've just been killed.

I brush him aside with a gesture of annoyance and dash into my office. My lieutenant, Lino, is there. Previously he had been a champion absenteeist, obstinately sticking to his dubious dealings, his bribe-taking and his whores. He had understood that in the sultanate of middlemen and nepotism, to obtain a miracle one had to negotiate for it. He earned next to nothing, never made a profit or benefited from any guarantee. As for housing, he didn't have an elastic enough asshole to obtain it; and family—he evidently had an intrepid penis, but not enough balls to start one. So that's how Lino coped, in the muddle that was our society.

In a country where you have to get up early to acquire a miserable fridge, one shouldn't make the sentry keep watch late. That is why, out of sympathy, I closed my eyes to his activities. But Lino wised up all of a sudden. He is at the office before the orderly. That's normal because he spends the night there. He no longer goes back home, to Bab el Oued, ever. Not since a trio of bearded guys came to measure his carotid in order to select an appropriate knife for the purpose. The lieutenant has been traumatized. He hardly dares to approach the window. And in the evening when he turns off the light to go to sleep he is so petrified that one can make out the ringing of his thoughts.

He is behind his typewriter, bluish rings on his clownish face. He has no more nails on his fingers, no more expression in his gaze, and he looks so pitiful it could melt a stone.

—Do you know what happens to guys who are too worried, Lino? They have bald children.

—I don't even know if I'll be in this world tomorrow.

—Stop wallowing in the role of victim! It makes absolutely no impression on anyone these days.... Have you read the BRQ Report?

—Yeah.

—Sum total?

—Two schools, one factory, a bridge, a communal park, forty-three electric pylons wrecked.

—And losses to human life?

—Three cops, a soldier on leave, a schoolteacher and four firemen.

—Why the firemen?

—The corpse they went to recover was booby-trapped.

—Ah, well…

I dig out a file that is gathering dust at the bottom of my drawer. A few ill-assorted pages, the photo of a Billy goat in an Afghan cassock, and a witch hunt which threatens to go on forever.

I gaze at the guru in the photo: twenty-eight years old. Never went to school. Never had work. Messianic peregrinations across Africa, preaching absolute virulence and an implacable hatred toward the entire world. And now here he was setting himself up as a righter of wrongs: thirty-four murders, two volumes of *fatwa,** a harem in every bush and a scepter on every finger. Verily, Hell doth burn solely by the flames of the divinely inspired.

I knew a small-time drug dealer. A repulsive excrescence, as much at ease in capital sin as a louse in a hippie's pants. Today he has a sawn-off shotgun, a verse on the tip of his tongue, and he gaily takes revenge on those who used to have him under their thumb.

May it not displease the revered *imams*, but if this excrement landed up in Paradise, I would have myself castrated by a plumber. Nonetheless, among the populace, he is considered a martyr. Ever since terrorism has put religion in the front rows of sedition, the simple folk don't know what to think. Everything that has an Islamist connotation disconcerts them. Instinctively, they survive the tragedy philosophically and refrain from dwelling on it. *Après moi le déluge*—the ancestral saying that didn't give a damn. And there is no worse solitude than that of a shipwrecked person.

One day, maybe, I shall be able to saunter about the boulevards of my city without a care in the world. One day, maybe, night will attend my slumber with touching confidences. I shall have kids around my paunch, and sunglasses on my face to make-believe that I'm on a cruise ship. I will be able to permit myself to go to the theater and laugh at my own disappointments, or else go to fetch my milk from the shopkeeper on the corner without fear of the onlookers. Only I do not think I shall gaze at my compatriots with the eyes of yesteryear. Something will have severed the mooring ropes of my home port. I will not feel spite—there isn't enough room in my sadness—but all the affected simpering of the funny girls will not be able to reconcile me with those whom I consider today to be my potential gravediggers.

For my friends, I shall have only mixed feelings, and my neighbors on my landing will be as unfamiliar to me as the Indians of Wyoming. The survivors of this filthy war will bawl in my brain, just like those phantoms that graves reject and houses refuse entry to, and which will remain suspended between heaven and earth, too guilty to draw near to God and too compromised to join with human beings.

Nothing will be as before. The songs which enthused me will no longer touch me. The breeze loitering in the recesses of the night will no longer gently rock my reveries. Nothing will equal the brightness of my rare moments of forgetfulness, for after what I have seen I will never again be a happy man.

I am still ruminating this bitter fodder when the orderly returns to remind me of the boss' impatience. With the delicacy of an elephant conscious of its approaching death, I tear my behind from the seat's embrace and painfully ascend the sixty-eight steps of the stairway—the elevator being reserved exclusively for the boss' personal use—to the third floor.

The boss spreads himself out behind his desk. Within the all-pervading luxury he has the air of a monument. But when seen close, the monument is more like a fairground freak astride the wrong column. He pays no attention to my cursory greeting. Without a word he pushes a bit of paper in my direction: I don't have time to deal with this, he announces to me before resuming the filing of his nails.

—What is it?

—The son-in-law of Monsieur Ghoul* Malek.

—The ex-star of the Republic? Has he been killed?

He starts, outraged. Then explains: He's inaugurating his new residence.

—And that's why he's contacting the Criminal Department?

—It's an invitation. I can't go. I've got things that prevent me going.

As I am not following him, he lights my lantern: You will represent me.

—Look, I've also got work, I have, I protest on the verge of vomiting at the idea of flirting with that low-life putrescence, born of a perjury, and whom I detest to an almost inconceivable degree.

—It's an order!

After which he swivels his chair round to offer me his back, broad as the Berlin wall. I conceive it thus in the hope of seeing it fall, along with him, too, but remain persuaded that miracles may only be reserved for good Christians.

Chapter two

I spend an hour rummaging through my clothing to unearth a clownish tie dating from before the nationalization of petroleum. Mina contemplates me in the mirror. From time to time she pats down a mutinous lock in my fleece, flicks away a grain of dust on my jacket, tender, attentive, too loving to recognize in me the air of a freed serf, which I nonetheless embody with great authenticity.

—It makes you look younger.

Probably; it's a suit that I used to wear in the days when the regime produced revolutions for us at every opportunity with the staggering dexterity of a conjurer. At that time the cheap synthetic fiber made one into a bourgeois socialist and the demagogues appreciated it even when their shiny alpaca verged on heresy.

I leap into my jalopy and tear along toward Hydra, the most chic neighborhood in the city. Hydra, in these competitive times, is reminiscent of a forbidden city. Never has a fundamentalist's beard ruffled its mimosas, never has the smell of gunpowder violated the fragrances of its felicity. The *nabobs** of the land live there as pensioners, with well-stocked paunches, their eye riveted on the prospect of profit. The wars of Algeria possess this impenetrable singularity that the belligerents are grossly in error as to whom their enemies are.

On his civil servant's pay-slip, Monsieur Ghoul Malek's son-in-law has just enough wherewithal to feed himself on sandwiches and to buy himself a dozen briefs on a five-year installment plan. Nonetheless, his new residence is on a par with Club Med: over three thousand square meters festooned with lanterns, garlands, balloons as obese as hot-air balloons. There is even a parking area specially arranged for the occasion. Luxury automobiles gleam as far as the eye can see. I park my ignoble Zastava between two Mercedes. Setting foot on the ground I have the impression that my wagon has shrunk.

Two towering hulks come over to make sure that I have not unexpectedly arrived from Lesotho. They check their list and are disconcerted to find that I appear on it. I linger for a few moments to admire the palace of the favored one: a ground floor to make an emir of Kuwait salivate, two floors to make me die twice over. How much overseas marble, how many murderous provocations!

I observe a minute's silence in the memory of the vows of the resistance members, of the martyrs of knowledge and of my ideals. Then, with the courage of forward flight, I mount a staircase that might easy blend in in Hollywood. It feels like the progress of someone who has been sentenced to death on the scaffold. A marionette with the air of an imported majordomo greets me as if he had been issued with an early morning fine. His eyebrows almost detach themselves at the sight of my grotesque get-up.

—Domestics, on the other side, he decrees stiffly.

—Well then, what are you doing around here?

Seeing that I am set to be stubborn, he claps his hand with a mystical gesture. Three ugly and evil-looking fellows appear, with armor-plated heads, and jaws that would intimidate the shock absorbers of a half-track.

—Superintendent Llob, I hasten, to brake their impulses.

This shocks the majordomo, who sighs, in deep consternation: Poor Algeria!

The salon is almost as vast as my bile. My ulcer spontaneously discovers an expansionist tendency. There's a big crowd. Each one bears his standing as, of yore, his groom of a father bore his master's saddle. I make a valiant effort to compare them to penguins, strapped as they are in their severe dinner jackets, but I cannot. They are so handsome, so elegant, so happy. No doubt about it, the world belongs to them; the sun rises only for them. The war, which is ravaging the country, hasn't enough courage to risk encroaching on their domain. To them it's simply subversion.

Among the guests I recognize several bigwigs, the millionaire Dahmane Faïd, Assembly deputies, Sid Lankabout* the writer, ladies decorated like Christmas trees, young women fit to make the stalk of an old Arab spring erect. And me, amid all of this, I have the air of a bug aboard a flying carpet. Useless to keep telling myself that at least I'm honest, that I have a clean conscience, that there is no blood on my savings; it's no good: however upright, however healthy I am, next to these people, I don't merit any more consideration than a doormat.

Emerging from among a train of Adonises, Sid Lankabout stops strutting on catching sight of me: "That was all we needed," I read on his lips.

—Well, well, coos a throat at my back, if it isn't our dear superintendent?

I pivot. It's Haj Garne.* His smile, that of a false devotee, turns my stomach.

Haj Garne is one of the most dangerous freebooters of our troubled territorial waters. A notorious sodomite, an exhaust pipe would give him ideas. Legend has it that our eminent devotee of the anal sciences fucks everything that moves except for the hands of a watch, all that stands upright except for the buoys, and everything that can be touched except for the minutes of a judicial report.

Instinctively, his viscous paw caresses my wrist before menacing the base of my back. I retreat, prudent. My age and my spinelessness would never provide me with protection adequate enough against his questionable habits.

—As plump as ever, steak house cop-chicken.

—It's my nerves.

He runs his fingers over his bandit whiskers, lingers over my peasant's Sunday-best disguise, and comments sadly:

—Your honesty has not got you very far, dear Superintendent. I hope you're managing to make ends meet.

—Now and again.

He sniggers.

Once again he eyes my old jacket, my crumpled trousers, my crooked shoes.

—Your problem, Llob, is stagnation. You have remained the same scarecrow as you were thirty years ago. It's distressing. When will you learn to take the long-term view?

—I haven't got a long enough nose.

He shakes his head, ports his lips to one side and grunts: You can't imagine what a sorry sight you make, old fellow. One day you won't even dare to look at yourself in the mirror. One doesn't spit at a passing train. One runs the risk of the spit being blown back into one's face.

He moves away.

A species of duchess spots me, makes me a little comma sign with the hand. I turn around to see if it's not directed at someone else. The duchess makes a 'no' with the end of her nose, points at me with an insistent finger. Then she unfurls her sperm whale carcass on me, proffering me her flipper:

—Oh! she rejoices, swaying like a serpent, Superintendent Llob, at last, here before me in the flesh. How I've longed to meet you! Do you know you're my favorite novelist?

—I didn't know that.

—Yes, oh yes. You are *the* best. You have such a great talent.

—That's because I don't have enough money.

—That's not true. It has nothing to do with it. (She steps back to stare at me). You are taking it to heart!

—First of all I have to have one.

She throws back her head in a laugh so huge that one can make out the designs on her chemise, then, touched by my look of frustrated envy, she takes my arm and presses it very hard against her breasts.

—Listen, Superintendent. I am planning to organize a gala, to launch my charitable society. I would be delighted to receive you among my friends.

—That's very kind of you, Madame.

—Lankabout, Fatima Lankabout, Sid's wife. Close friends call me "Fa," like the cosmetics brand. One more thing, Superintendent, I beg of you to forgive my lack of discretion; women, we're like that, but frankly: are you an autodidact?

—Only autochthonous.

She devours me with her eyes. There is no doubt about it, I fascinate her. But I'd rather desecrate a mausoleum than reveal to her the hidden part of the iceberg. I gratify her with a chaste smile and hasten to merge in among the privileged fauna. Ghoul Malek's son-in-law falls on me with the voracity of a praying mantis.

—You came after all, he exults. Your boss was skeptical, but I was sure that you would show up. You might have principles, but there appears to be no leash on your curiosity.

—A professional defect.

—Well, (he displays his empire to me) what do you think of it? Do you like it, my ghetto?

—Please don't put yourself out. In the land of impunity the sharks owe it to themselves to take double mouthfuls.

He laughs, catches me by the elbow and drags me in his wake.

—Come, I shall introduce you to my friends. There might just be a benevolent dry cleaner among them.

I just have time to adjust my turban and he is already exhibiting me like some surrealist trophy before a band of prevaricators who seem inordinately proud of their corpulence.

—Sirs, I have the pleasure of introducing to you the cleverest, most outstanding cop in the land.

They barely notice my presence, these neo-beys of Algiers.

My revered father used to say that there is no worse tyrant than a minder of asses who has turned sultan. Shepherds yesterday, dignitaries today, the notables of my land have amassed colossal fortunes but they will never succeed in separating from the rest of the herd. The biggest one turns round and growls ill humoredly.

—Is that it, your San Antonio?

The stockiest one permits himself the display of a contemptuous rictus and asks me: How do you manage to sustain your smile above such a hopeless looking tie, Superintendent?

—It's enough for me to observe you.

His Highness is not appreciative. He warns me: Be careful, you're addressing a deputy.

I eye him with disdain. If he thinks to benefit from his parliamentary idiot's immunity with me, then he is being exceedingly optimistic.

My host jerks me into a corner and gives me a lesson.

—Easy, Llob, my guests have long arms.

—I knew that they had something in common with chimps.

—Idiot! I give you the chance to make some solid contacts, and you behave...

—I have an ulcer, I interrupt him.

—So?

—My physician advised me against eating that bread.

—You prefer the black?

—Absolutely.

—Very well then, stay with it.

Upon which he abandons me in favor of a corrupt mayor.

I don't feel at all at ease. I try to acclimatize myself, but it's not easy. The fairytale universe is bathed by the music, and now and again nibbled at by the languorous laughter of some fat, tipsy, hags; the superb automobiles are paraded across the park like sacred cows; the splendor and pretentiousness of the vips is boundless; the full moon in the azure sky, the self-satisfied rustle of fortunes—everything in the place makes me want to puke. This isn't the Algeria I know.

In my country the cemeteries never cease to fill with tears and blood, the honest folk scrape the walls to guard against the evil eye...yet here in this Taj Mahal for vengeful eunuchs, everything is fine and dandy. Not a trace of difficulty, not the slightest sense of insecurity. The pirates of my homeland have made themselves a watertight and disinfected microcosm, and never did greased poles seem to me more imposing than the monuments in these places of prosperity.

I collect my naive complexes, climb into my chariot, purposely bumping the wing of a large sedan—unfortunately it's my Zastava which comes off the worse—and slip away as best I can toward the city heights in search of a breath of air, vitiated no doubt, but at least less contaminated.

Chapter three

I am in my misshapen armchair and I watch the dawn taking its time to rise. The shots and the sirens have not stopped hurling invective at one another the whole night long. Flames have devoured a depot on the heights of the quarter. A bomb exploded behind the hill. Next came this damned draught of air which teases the noisy spirits of my apartment block and which obliges me to remain on my guard until the morning.

From my window I can see the itching misery of the *Casbah*, its murky blackness, and, at the end, the Mediterranean. There was a time when, from my vantage point of 'zealous patriot,' it seemed to me that nobility was born from these hovels, bruised and battered by the war and disappointments, that my alleyways with their parchment configurations contained the essence of valor. It was a time when Algiers possessed the whiteness of doves and innocence, where, in our children's eyes the horizons of the earth saw their virginity restored. It was the time of slogans, of chauvinism; the time when the Lie, more adept than a mythical ancient, knew how to court us, while the evening went to bed on a day of distressing emptiness.

Today, from beneath the ruins of abuse, the Nation raises its robes to reveal terrifying deformities, and the most horrifying of barbarities cannot rival the ugly excesses of my proud haven.

Henceforth in my country, almost to the point of no return, there are kids whom they machine-gun simply because they go to school, and young girls they decapitate because one must strike fear in others. Henceforth in my country, with some prayers to the good Lord, there are days that get up simply to go away, and nights which are only black when we have to identify ourselves to our consciences. But what can one expect from a system which, the day after its independence, hastened to rape the widows and the orphans of its own martyrs?

Mina wriggles beneath the covers. Her virginal voice reaches me in a sleepy breath: Come to bed.

—It's six AM.

She raises herself on an elbow, pours at me a look of bewilderment: You worry me.

—You're right to be worried. I haven't taken any out life insurance.

Answering her, I am conscious of my spitefulness, but can't help it. I know that I risk my skin every day and it gives me the shits.

ॐ

Lino intercepts me on the threshold of the station. There is a spider's web on the right-hand lens of his glasses.

—I trod on it, he admits, in order to arouse a semblance of my compassion.

—That proves that you are still standing on your feet.

With his stress-racked finger he indicates the waiting room: Ait Meziane has been waiting for you for an hour already.

—The great comedian? I inquire enthusiastically.

The Ait Meziane who is moping in the waiting room in no way resembles the performer upon whom all the footlights were trained: a pitiful, washed out remnant of a man, as faceless as his shadow, he has the night on his face.

He stares at the toes of his shoes, with his fingers inextricably locked.

—What has got you in such a state? I say, attempting to put him at his ease.

He hands me an envelope. Without saying a word.

It's a threatening letter, signed "Abou Kalybse."* It warns the performer not to go anywhere near the theater, to stop frequenting these "aides of Satan" of intellectuals, and to pay the mufti, in the guise of a contribution, the modest sum of 100,000 dinars. I sit down facing him, trying maladroitly:

—This must surely be a practical joke.

Meziane manages a derisory smile:

—Do you find that people here make jokes?

I am embarrassed. People in his situation are legion. At the beginning they were provided with discreet police surveillance, which tried to keep an eye on the vicinity, then, with the demand becoming increasingly heavy, and our losses more and more stinging, everyone tries to look out for himself and to rely on the blundering of the executioners.

—You know me, Llob. We were brats together, rubbing the bottoms of our pants on the same sidewalks. I am not one to sound the alarm the moment a flea appears on my pillow. But this time I have the feeling that my smile is liable to vanish altogether.

I nod gently, incapable of offering a comforting word.

—I don't engage in politics. I steer clear of controversy. I only fight for laughter, Llob. My sole desire is to remove tension, to entertain...

—Above all, don't search for any reprehensible attitude in yourself, Ait. That's not what motivates them.

—What should I do? he asks impatiently. My suitcase or my prayer?

—Let's not give way to panic. There must surely be a way. You have friends in Oran, or else in Constantine. Get yourself lost for a bit and wait for the storm to blow over.

—They will find me and kill me.

—Leave the country....

—No, he cries. Don't ask me to exile myself in Europe. It's true, they are safe, the people on the other bank, but I am incapable of vegetating at more than twenty kilometers from my housing project. In any case, I don't know myself why I came to bother you, overwhelmed as you are.

He rises. Like a curtain on a stage of shame. The wings of his scorched soul seem to me all at once as opaque as the depths of the sea…I feel ashamed to see him depart like this, disappointed and lost, like a hope torn to shreds at a time when consciences are fossilized.

❧

When Ghoul Malek ordered me to come and see him at 13 rue des Pyramides, I nearly drowned in my glass. An influential member of the old, ruling oligarchy, Malek had been a particularly feared big brother in the days of the single party. When he appeared on TV, it was enough to make people want to barricade themselves behind their curtains. Among his prerogatives were: the summary execution of 'undesirables,' changing the laws, making women abort, and aborting social projects; in short, he had the power of day and night.

Since the hysteria of October 1988* he has cultivated the impression of having retired from the fray. In reality, he continues to pull the strings from his majestic property at Hydra, and even though he no longer appears on the TV screens, his reputation of bogeyman still haunts people's minds.

Consequently, when his voice rang out at the other end of the line—if you'll pardon the expression—something froze in my underpants.

I arrive at 13 rue des Pyramides a little before ten PM. It's raging with rain. Flashes of slightly schizoid lightning hurl their anathema over a supremely impassible Hydra. I maneuver my go-cart onto the stone path of a fir-lined alley and roll for about a hundred meters before reaching the palace. It takes me a hell of a time to locate the doorbell among the multitude of buttons ornamenting the control panel at the entrance. The door opens to reveal an albino gorilla.

—I'm Superintendent L—
—Wipe your shoes on the doormat!
The tone is authoritarian, staggeringly hostile.

18

Calmly, I wipe my old shoes on the doormat. Just as I am about to hang up my coat, the gorilla stops me hastily...

—You can keep it, Monsieur. The interview won't take long.

—I hope so, Snow White, I hope so.

My hot blood changes to nitroglycerin. This does not impress the animal who, after a withering glance, takes off toward a padded door.

I relax by interesting myself in the luxury encircling me like a prisoner's iron collar; notice an African statuette, go to examine it more closely.

—Watch out for the alarm, snaps a voice behind me.

Monsieur Ghoul Malek is standing in the middle of the hall, elephantine. He resembles Orson Welles—without his talent. He is wearing a vast scarlet dressing gown and holds a cigar between his fingers, one of which sports a ring as big as a shellfish. I sketch a purely professional smile and extend a hand that remains suspended shamefully in thin air.

The old party boss walks around me, then bends over the statuette.

—You left too quickly, the other evening, from my son-in-law's place.

—My tie was bothering me, monsieur.

He hems and haws, then, referring to the statuette:

—I shall never understand why such a timeworn object costs the earth.

—The vagaries of fortune, I presume, Monsieur Malek.

I saw that he started, but hid it well.

—Do you know anything about the plastic arts, Superintendent?

—I manage now and again to tell the difference between Salvador Dali and a house painter.

He shakes his head:

—They say that you are religious, Monsieur Llob.

—It makes one feel good.

—Islamist?

—Moslem.

—Well, well…

—Monsieur, it's after 10 AM, and I would like to get home before the curfew.

Calmly he turns around, stares at me:

—They also say that you are a good detective.

—That proves that they talk too much.

He suddenly plants a photo under my nostrils:

—My daughter, Sabrine.

—She's beautiful.

—She has disappeared.

I nod gently. For no apparent reason. Probably out of one-party habit.

—Does she ever leave home?

—She had no reason to do so.

—I see. How long since she disappeared?

—Three or four weeks.

—She isn't with friends, relatives?

—Superintendent, (he is already tiring), I chose you because I don't want this affair to be public knowledge, for one thing. Secondly, my daughter never goes absent without leaving a contact number. She also knows how to use a phone.

—I think—

—Thank you, Superintendent, you can leave.

The flour-covered gorilla is there at once to see me out.

—I am sorry, but a photo by itself just doesn't—

—It's sufficient when one is a good detective. Good evening.

Indolent pachyderm, he disappears behind the padded door.

—Follow me, burps the albino at me at the nape of my neck.

I follow him. Docile. Once on the threshold I take out a ten-dinar note and slip it into his pocket: Buy yourself a less troubling air, Monsieur Yeti.

Quite unperturbed, the albino takes the note and stuffs it into my mouth. I don't have time to catch him: the door slams in my face.

Chapter four

The Limbes Rouges is a cabaret hidden away in the corner of the rue des Lauriers Roses. Frequented by spoiled Algerian tramps, it offers a glittering bar, a spacious dance floor, nicely decorated tables and perfectly discrete recesses. They serve imported liquors there, stuffed pheasant and, if you enjoy the reverie of artificial paradises, joints of hashish that can make you forget your troubles. Since it is a guarded shrine, one encounters there high officials with a fondness for virgin boys—which is why one notices a surreptitious odor of Vaseline in the air, sexy ladies, and a bevy of interesting characters. The menu is copious, and the bill fantastic. If you are not a white-collar worker and you aren't known at the door, there's no chance of being admitted.

A gigolo with steroid-pumped-up muscles stands guard at the entrance. As soon as he spots me he almost faints, so out of place do I appear in those parts: Hey! Horse dealer, he barks. The livestock market is on the other side of town.

I pay no attention to his yapping, push past him and enter the den of the incubi. Waiters are circulating everywhere. In silence.

It's nice. On the velvety walls, there are pornographic scenes, little lamps with phallic contours—all very stimulating.

A near-naked woman emerges through a curtain, with an unattractive face and her hair in a severe bun. She deploys her viper's charms on me. My umbilical starter having become blocked long ago, her smile leaves me quite unmoved.

—What can I do for you? she whistles point blank.

—For me not much, but for her.... (I show her Sabrina's picture). It seems she frequents this place.

—She's not the only one.

—Do you recognize her?

—Should I...?

—She hasn't returned home.

—It isn't among our duties to see our clients home. Is that all, Inspector?

—Superintendent. Superintendent Llob.

My glory makes not the slightest impression on her, the ignoramus.

—Excuse me. We open in less than three hours and I have two teams to put to work.

Without waiting for my permission, she goes back inside her curtain.

—Now scram, and make it quick! growls the gigolo with the steroid-enhanced muscles.

And he bundles me straight to the exit. At my age!

—Well? inquires Lino as he starts the engine of the department car.

—Like looking for an honest butcher in the month of Ramadan.

—What are we going to do?

—What do you suggest?

※

The Cinq Etoiles is a brand new hotel. All bay windows with stained glass. With its eleven floors overhanging the hill and the city it resembles a futuristic mausoleum. They say that at the start a hospital was envisaged, but that by the time they reached the sixth story the good intentions ran out of breath. Characters in high places got into the act. Before the ninth story the documents changed hands and content radically, to the extent that at the dedication, instead of the national anthem, the guests were treated to a delightful evening of popular Algerian *rai* music. The result: the poor continue to die in unbelievably filthy pigsty-like dispensaries.... Bah! what good does it do me to bring her back, me, a roast chicken cop, a big mouth in a pinhead for whom the only fitting status is that of a cardboard target.

Transcendent bosom and splendid young face, Mademoiselle Anissa is the stuff of dreams. Her gaze does not falter when under siege. Her smile, simple as *bonjour*, would make a legless man run faster than the curfew siren. She receives us in her suite, graciously ceded by a philanthropist and pro-youth administrator—the kind that this good old Algeria knows how to dispatch.

—Yes? she chirps, settling herself generously on to a sofa.

—She went missing at roll call.

—Who?

—Sabrine Malek.

—I know about it. Her father's chauffeur came to see me, a few days ago.

—What did he want?

—He thought she was my friend.

—Wasn't she your friend?

—My clients are sufficient for me.

Lino scribbles something on his pad. He pretends to take this seriously.

—Do you know Sabrine's father?

—He has an albino chauffeur who drives a Mercedes.

—That's all?

—That's all.

I look at Lino and Lino looks at his pad.

—What exactly is your profession?

—The oldest in the world.

This makes the lieutenant's ears prick up his ears; sufficiently for him to raise his head.

—Did Sabrine engage in that profession?

—I don't think so. She is a spoiled daughter. She loves to mess her world up. I am sure that she is just around somewhere planning to watch people go to pieces. She's an unstable one, Sabrine.

Then her gaze, like that of an inflatable doll, alights on the clock and she simpers:

—But I'm late, Superintendent. I have to get myself ready. This evening there will be a lot of people and I have to hurry to be in the front row.

—When did you see her last?

—Hard for me to remember, she says rising. Why don't you ask at the Limbes Rouges?

—The proprietress claims that she doesn't remember her.

—That's bizarre. I thought they were Siamese twins.

We go back, Lino and me, to the rue des Lauriers Roses. The proprietress barely avoids swallowing her dentures when I surprise her in the throes of changing, with her breasts exposed.

—Look, this isn't a public thoroughfare! she protests.

—Because it's a brothel.

—I beg you, Superintendent, a little propriety.

—I won't make you say it.

The Bonzo on duty tries to pull my ear. I feint with my left and punch him in the molars. Flabbergasted by my emergency procedure, the tart-de-luxe opens her mouth as if to receive a horse's member.

—What is it you want then?

—To continue with my inquiry.

—Have you got a warrant?

—Only a check without coverage.

She gets excited, grabs a phone and dials a familiar number.

—Eh! Are you calling the police?

—Better still, Superintendent, I'm calling your chief.

—That's all!

—I won't insist.

There's just time to administer another one-two on the

gigolo—to prove to myself that I am not the last of the last—and I beat a hasty retreat.

࿐

In the afternoon Ghoul Malek calls me. He is not in a pleasant mood. For a moment I expect to see his hand spring from within the receiver to take me by the throat. Lino, who caught sight of me standing in for a chameleon, at once thought that I was having a heart attack.

—Are you feeling ill, Super?

With my free hand I order him to keep silent while I shake my head obsequiously, emitting an interminable rosary of "Very good, Monsieur."

—I want to see you here in thirty minutes, thunders the ex-divinity.

—Very good, Monsieur.... At once. Monsieur...I'm on my way, Monsieur.

The albino gorilla opens the door. He is decidedly unhappy to see us. With an unenthusiastic hand he unhooks a microphone and announces:

—Superintendent Llob, Monsieur, he is not alone.... Very good, Monsieur.

He replaces the mike and points to a corridor.

—Straight ahead.

I pass. Lino, however, is unlucky. As he is about to enter, the albino catapults him backward.

—Not you, lackey. Only the stuck-up old fool.

I prime my left, but my courage has different ideas apparently, as I feel a tinge of yellow about the gills. Lino is sad. He looks like a brat who's been refused admission to the movie house.

—Let him at least wait in the salon, I protest.

—Is he disinfected?

—What?

—In that case he'll wait outside.

And he disappears. I can hear Lino moan outside the door. Poor pup, my heart bleeds for him.

Ghoul Malek is reclining on a wicker chair, beside a clover-

25

shaped pool. His gross popular bloodsucker's paunch pours onto his knees. On hearing me shuffling my shoes on the paving of the path, he camouflages himself behind sunglasses and raises a Cuban cigar to his sewer mouth.

—Sorry about your companion, I did not ask to see him.

—He's one of my team, a police officer!

The audacious tone of my discontentment displeases him. Quite evidently he is not given to tolerating vexing remarks. He removes his glasses and dispatches me a look so significant that I feel my ancient buttocks turning to jelly.

—You will have to stuff your head in a damned fridge, Superintendent.

—Why, Monsieur?

—To refresh your memory. I remind you that I insisted on the most absolute discretion.

—He's my lieutenant.

—Get rid of him.

After a mortal silence, he trumpets: One more thing; don't even think of returning to the Limbes Rouges. It's selective and very discreet. In any case, my men have tried that path and didn't turn up anything. And don't go looking at my side of the family either. I have an envious brother and prejudiced cousins, and Sabrine is totally unaware of their existence.

—All that remains for me is to solicit the goodwill of a tarot card reader, Monsieur.

—That's your problem.

—Is your daughter in any danger?

His features regroup themselves around an outraged grimace on his face:

—What is danger, Superintendent?

He puts his glasses back on and ignores me. The interview is over.

The albino practically marches me out, *manu militari*. Once on the steps, I point to his jacket. He lets himself be taken in by this age old game for simpletons, and lowers his head to see what it's all about; I profit from this and give him a finger flick on the nose.

Instead of playing fair, the sod throws his right hook into my gimpy leg and sends me pirouetting down the steps.

Lino runs to help me up.

The albino eyes us with contempt for a moment before closing the door.

—He took me by surprise, I explain to Lino.

—That's it, sympathizes my subordinate.

—One day, I promise you, I shall boot that milky yak's ass.

Lino is good enough to nod agreement to his chief. Though without much conviction.

Chapter five

Bliss Nahs* is what might be termed the station seismograph. When he is twiddling his thumbs behind his desk, it's a good sign: one can sip one's tea unconcernedly. On the other hand, when he is excoriating the other departments, one buttock on a corner of the table, mouth spewing out sinister anecdotes, that means a bad die has been cast. The fellow is a mosquito, quite untamable. As is the case with many losers, for want of excelling at anything else, he excels at being a killjoy. I suspect the boss of having burdened me with him solely to keep an eye on me. Ever since he has had this evil augury trailing in my wake, I can no longer flush the toilet without the hierarchy being aware of it. This morning Bliss is out of control, making me hasten to spit beneath my shirt to ward off the evil spirits.

Lino feigns tidying his shelves with the manifest intention of avoiding the splatterings of bad luck. An incurable fatalist, Inspector Serdj mutters incantations. Baya the secretary is in a state of shock; she has just noticed that her pocket mirror is cracked.

—Superintendent, howls Bliss, you are not going to believe…

I wave my hand in front of my face on account of the breath of the dispenser of pessimism.

—Haven't got time!

His enthusiasm evaporates at once:

—I am not a leper, damn it! I have my self-esteem.

—Try another washing powder, old man, because it's not very clean.

—I have the right to the same consideration as my other colleagues. It's not right to treat me in this way. We're at war, damn it! We have to stick together.

And he returns to his niche, like a mist descending when the bright intervals grow too bold.

—I was beginning to get a stiff neck, groans Lino, emerging from behind his barricade. That owl will perforate my ulcer one of these days. Say, Super, can't you get him reassigned far away from here?

—Impossible. He has a sister in the administration and she lets herself be fucked front and back.

Baya acts confused, taking refuge behind her hands.

I motion to my slaves to follow me. Once we are alone, I wait for their reports.

Because he is the ranking senior and the most ambitious, Lino begins first. He flicks through his pad. I know there is nothing in it, but this bluff has the merit of reducing my nervous tension.

—Sabrine Malek, blonde, green eyes…damn, where did I put it, where is it…? Ah, here it is…page nineteen. The girl has a jet engine in her behind. She can't stay still in one place. At high school her sultry looks didn't earn her high marks for intelligence.

—She was last seen three weeks ago, continues Serdj. She was with a certain Mourad Atti, a pimp during his out-of-penitentiary hours.

—According to her school chums, she was always playing truant. She never finished her courses. She was a girl with problems. She wasn't much liked.

—I want you to find that Mourad At—

I haven't finished the sentence when a tremendous explosion

rocks the building. Immediately all hell breaks loose around us. Lino is petrified, his glasses shaking on the end of his nose. I push past Serdj and dash into the corridor. From up in his third story the director is shouting. No one hears him. Everyone is running toward the courtyard, purple in the face and with shivers down the spine.

Outside, an anemic sky consents to piece the clouds together. In the street, the idlers watch the drama without realizing it. A black plume of smoke stripes the facades. Broken bodies bleed on the sidewalk.

—Car bomb, stammers the policeman on guard. The young boy, he flew like a spark.

Someone yells to call for ambulances. These cries bring us to our senses. People emerge from their stupor, with wounds, horrors revealed. Panic reigns. In minutes the sun veils its face and the night—all of the night—settles in the very midst of the morning.

⁊

Mina has made me onion soup. It's my favorite dish. I am seated at the table, silent, and I stare at my plate without seeing it. The idea of breaking bread makes me nauseous. All I have to do is to close my eyes for the car bomb to explode in my head and for its shockwave to once more invade my calves.

I cannot recall who it was who brought me home. All I remember is that I could not get my Zastava to start. The spectacle of the torn bodies, of the child's contorted limbs on the pothole, unhinged me.

I have seen a lot of cadavers in my bitch of a career. When you see enough, you get used to it. But a dead infant, that's against nature. I shall never get over it entirely. Mina was good enough not to ask me any questions. She has learned not to probe me in times of misfortune.

My youngsters are in the salon. They avoid sitting at the table or engaging in conversation with me. They are intimately familiar with my moodswings, and they begrudge me for messing up their rare moments of respite. My daughter is nervous as soon as I arrive. It's sufficient for me to clear my throat for her to withdraw into her

31

shell. There is no greater frustration for me than to see my kids jump when I simply try to ask for a glass of water. Filthy war.

I push my plate away, run into my room. Mina joins me there. Her eyes are movingly reproachful. She settles at my back, massages my neck. Generally, when Mina catches me in this manner, I find it therapeutic. This evening every one of her touches seems to bruise me like a bite. I turn toward the window. The night secretes its bile over the city. Already, in the distance, a burst of fire unleashes the delirium.

Chapter six

It's a good two hours that I've been wearing down my elbows on the grimy counter of a café, at the corner of the rue des Revolutions. Perched on top of a stool, I warm a long-since tepid cup of tea between my hands. My watch reads eight-thirty in the evening and Mourad Atti is taking a long time to show. Lino is sitting at a table in a corner, squeezed into a worn overall that makes him look like an idle bricklayer. He is sitting on nettles, Lino. The neighborhood is not reputed for its tenderness to cops.

The cafe proprietor is a shriveled fellow. It seems to take him more time to serve a customer than it takes a local customs officer to let a passenger go. He might look debonair but for a nasty porcupine on his chops: a subversive beard that renders his proximity hazardous. Around me, a band of old timers converse while methodically cleaning out their nostrils. Further along, some adolescents are training their peepers on the scene: dismal beyond description. They have low eyebrows and aggressive lips, and they suffer their exclusion like a difficult pregnancy.

Nine o'clock!

I go to phone Mina to reassure her. On my return I discover

an individual comfortably installed in my place, his paws already around my cup.

—Heh! he jeers, Whoever goes hunting, loses his place.

—Yeah, but when he returns he chases off his dog!

With his finger he acknowledges that I have made a point and removes his large posterior from my stool. The cafe proprietor does not appreciate this. He scrubs the counter before me ill-humoredly and seizes the opportunity to confiscate my beverage.

Lino points to his watch, in order to remind me that the curfew is still in force. I signal him to keep a low profile.

Mourad Atti shows at last, a satchel under his arm. He greets a cigarette vendor who has chosen to deploy his gear of misery on the café doorstep, inspects the vicinity, lingers on me, then on Lino. We have aroused his suspicions, but he hasn't got time to make a getaway. Serdj pounces on him at once.

—Gently does it, Serdj murmurs to him.

Mourad attempts a diversion. I shut him up with my gun. In a flash we have him bouncing on the back seat of the station Peugeot and we roar away on the hubcaps of the wheels. The manner in which the locals have viewed our maneuver cautions me against ever setting foot in that neighborhood again.

⁂

Haj Garne has no need of a truth serum to betray himself; he is the incarnation of falsehood par excellence. His smile, his bursts of laughter, his greasy slaps on the shoulder—are all nothing but a lure. Garne belongs to that stratum of sub-humanity that has got on and succeeded in spite of never having divested itself of its lice-ridden origin. Multidisciplinary illiterate, he albeit takes great pains to give himself an appearance on par with his fortune. Unfortunately, that benighted past is there at the end of the gesture, loutish, savage, evoking a circus monkey whose bellboy costume fails to hide the grimaces.

—I wasn't expecting to see you here, he exclaims, giving me a vicious hug.

—I came to wade in your muck.

—I thought you might have.

To the best of my knowledge Garne once slaved away as an ironworker for a colonist. How he ever succeeded in building his empire is a real Chinese puzzle. He never took a risk. During the 1954–1962 war he scrupulously held on to his blowlamp. After Independence, he managed to get himself a municipal registration card and registered in a trade union. The militants adopted him with alacrity, and it was in their viper's nest that he was initiated into the strategies of intrigue and dubious dealings.

Every time I try to grasp the lesson of such an irony, I deduce from it that an ill-met inversion of the pages of History makes Algerian society unfit for evaluation.

—I might as well tell you right away that you are not welcome in my home, he warns me.

—I thought that might just be the case.

He doesn't give ground to let me through:

—What is your problem, Cop? Doesn't your rear end ache when your hen lays eggs?

—It's mainly someone else's hen that makes me shit.

—You have the right to be polygamous. So then, just *what* is your problem?

—I'm growing old.

—There are old age homes, you know? You're not looking for my pity, I presume. Around here, you haven't got a hope. I've got no sympathy for cops.

—No, I haven't come for your pity, Haj.

—If you've come to pull the devil by the tail, try not to get the wrong side.

He gives me a menacing look. Well then?

—Mourad Atti says that he works for you.

—Who is that idiot??

—A pimp.

—I've got a whole contingent of them. So what?

—He was using a girl who has disappeared, a certain Sabrine Malek.

He curls the corner of his mouth:

35

—Look here, my newborn chick. Your kind, who mess up people's plans, don't bother me in the least. As for your insinuations—just forget them. For your information, I cheat twice as much as I breathe. I have a finger in every cesspool, and a nose in anything that produces a profit. I am a living monument to rottenness. And I infuriate you. You imbecile! Don't you realize that your cop badge is only there so people can recognize you?! Because you're insignificant. Because that's the way it is; like it or lump it.

I told you, didn't I, that he is a rustic. No more courtesy than a wooden club. It has to be acknowledged that the country harbors a whole load of lads like him, convinced that the law is for others; lads so sure of their impunity that the sight of a policeman is perceived by them as an anomaly, a vague déjà vu.

I turn around toward Lino who had remained in the Peugeot, feverishly wiping my brow with a handkerchief.

—You have given me a real shock you know, I admit. Ah! there, there, you have just made me burst a valve. I have never been so severely reduced to silence. Damn! I'm dripping from it like a Camembert...do I presume that I shall not extract anything worthwhile from this interview?

—Indeed. What's more, consider yourself lucky to extract yourself from it so cheaply.

He climbs the three steps of his stair, pauses before adding: Next time, Superintendent, phone first. I prefer to receive peasants in a canteen so as not to make them feel out of place. Here at home, I receive only my friends.

—I shall remember that, I promise.

He slams the door behind him.

Lino guesses that I have been rapped across the knuckles, and for once he makes out as if nothing happened. Without asking questions, he moves off, looking straight ahead, like a big boy. After about a hundred meters I order him to put the car into reverse. There again he asks no questions and performs. Like a big boy.

I ring Haj Garne's doorbell again and don't even give him time to see who it is. Barely has he shown his face when I expedite my right just on the spot where his lovers coo their intimacies to him.

He collapses like an awning and lands in the hallway, open-mouthed, with his arms crossed.

Satisfied, I adjust my coat, massage my fist and rejoin Lino who is already imagining me crucified on the altar of sacrileges.

꽃

On seeing me enter, the boss replaces his legs on the desk. In the conventional pantomime, this signifies that I am not worth more than a pile of dung on a waste ground. After a pregnant silence he trumpets:

—When are you going to wise up, Llob? A damn good evening! When will you learn not to bite the neighbor as soon as you're let off the leash? We're not in the Wild West…

I stay silent. In accordance with articles 13 and 69 of the regulations of the National Criminal Investigation Department, which stipulate: "When a chief lathers you, unworthy subaltern, you shut your trap so as not to foam inside and get diarrhea."

—A person can't go home anymore with you. One no longer has the right to an hour's relaxation. As soon as my back is turned you find a way to turn the city upside down.

—I didn't quite get the story of the leash, Monsieur le directeur.

—How come you dared to lift a hand against the honorable Haj Garne?

—It was while I was trying to wipe my nose, Monsieur le directeur. I am horribly clumsy when I have a cold.

Seems to me that I went a bit too far because the chief stands up and bangs on the table. Since there is nevertheless justice on earth, he misses the blotter and his porcelain fist smashes onto the ashtray. I let him lick his damaged fingers, taut as a cord, his chin at 90 degrees. The director recovers some of his color as the pain gradually diminishes. He roars:

—He's going to lodge an official complaint. I shall do nothing to dissuade him. And I shan't lend you my umbrella again. Because I want to see the sky fall on your head, Llob. For some time you have been looking for your master, and now you have finally found him….

His nasal voice fatigues me. It's difficult to intimidate a brave spirit when one speaks through one's nose. I patiently endure my suffering. However much I take an interest in a couple of sparrows on a line in the yard, there's no way I can fly away.

The director reins in his diatribe. He mops himself up on a piece of silk. After catching his breath he makes me a proposition: You will phone him right away to offer him your apologies.

—Absolutely not.

—Did I hear right?

—Absolutely.

—Is this a mutiny?

—It's you who sees it that way.

—You are going to phone him right away or I shall compel you to do so!

—Ah, well!

I glare disdainfully at my giant with the feet of clay, take a deep breath and let loose:

—Fuck you and your ancestors, Monsieur product of nepotism. I knew you when you were pitiful in your garret, at Place 1er Mai, in your pillbox, whistling after the wagons. I also recall your scuffed pants and your scarecrow jacket. The vertigo of hierarchy has gone to your head. You'll have to be careful about vertigo.

—Don't address me with such familiarity! I'm your chief! You know I won't have it—

—I didn't even vote for you. If it were up to me, you wouldn't even deserve to appear on a lost property list. You are nothing, just a windy myth, a preserved fruit of mediocrity, an abundant little shit, an ingrate and a fat hypocrite…. As for your protégé, tell him that even if he is dying from hunger, a cop has self-respect.

I leave him planted in the peat bog of unvarnished truth about himself and slam the door behind me. In the corridor, the personnel, who have heard, congratulate me with their eyes or a gesture of the finger, incredulous and admiring.

Lino recovers after the flood. He is in seventh heaven. He plunges the appendage that passes for his nose into a rag and trumpets so hard that Baya in the next door room leaps up startled.

—They tell that you've just shut up the director, he exclaims, jubilant. Is it true that you called him a little shit?

—What about it?

—*Putain!* He exclaims in ecstasy. Where do you find them, your flaming expletives, Super?

—In the urinals.

Chapter seven

I went to see Da Achour. When I'm out of sorts, it's to him that I direct my steps. His serenity calms me down. He's a visionary, Da Achour, a prophet perhaps. He looks at the world as one looks into the eyes of someone one knows well. He always knows which way the wind is blowing, where the storm is bound for and, above all, he knows there is nothing one can do about it.

He lives at the exit of a phantom village, to the east of Algiers. A retreat completely devoted to renunciation, hidden away in a bend of beach, so recalcitrant and so secluded that even the terrorists are reluctant to lay siege to it. In the past it was a beautiful village frequented by prosperous French colonialists. There were lots of parasols with vibrant colors. The ice-cream salesmen offered glasses of lemonade as tall as towers. The municipal orchestra played Tino Rossi in the square, and inexperienced young girls willingly let themselves be grazed by the naughty antics of the local youth.

Then came the war, and the geraniums disappeared. Nothing remains of that ex-haven of fairs except for mean houses, a ripped up road and the feeling of counting for nothing. A few odd fishermen still cling to a jetty rejected by the waves, hidden by rotting reeds.

Da Achour haunts a hovel at the end of a path flanked by a hedge in disgrace and a pair of dogs so slow to react that they appear to be constipated. If not for a scrap of sea in the guise of the horizon and a stretch of cliff which serves as the sole homeport, one could think oneself in limbo.

Da Achour never leaves his rocking chair. For him it's a natural extension. A cigarette in the corner of his mouth, stomach resting on his tortoise legs, he stares untiringly at some undefined point in the distance. He is there, from morning to night, a song of El Anka within reach of his somnolence, quietly consuming his eighty years in a country that disappoints. He's been in quite a few wars, from Normandy to Dien Bien Phu, from Guernica to Djudjuras, and still cannot fathom why men prefer to have their faces smashed, when simply getting soused would suffice to bring them closer to each other.

Now Da Achour no longer interrupts his siesta. He is on the lookout, between two breakers, for the Lady with the silvery scythe. His wife passed away a generation ago, he has no offspring and would not be in the least troubled if the Good Lord would deign to summon him.

I find him on the veranda, feet up on the little one-legged table, eyeing the distance. His crimson nape shudders at the crunch of my soles. He doesn't turn around to see me cram myself onto a camp bed next to the railing. After a long interval, irritated by my sighs, he growls bad-temperedly: You've missed your vocation, Llob.

—Lino thinks that I would have made a good prompter in the theater, I admit.

—Better: you would have made an excellent coffee grinder…

—How so?

—Because you never stop looking at the dark side of things.

I observe the flight of a fully satiated butterfly, then refocus on the old man's striated nape:

—It's no fun, Da.

—You are *not* the Messiah.

—But I am worried.

—Listen, it's a waste of time short-circuiting the nerve cells.
I lean on my elbow.

—You can't see much from your rat hole, Da.

—Look Llob, whoever sees from afar, sees better.

—One cannot just sit and look on when our country is dis-
integrating.

—It's biological. The world is in process; it's undergoing the
metabolism of its senility. We are entering an era of mystic ecstasy,
the millennium of the gurus. Entire civilizations will be swept away
by a tremendous tide, returning to the points from where they issued.
The frontiers will be eroded, then completely swept away, the races
and the basic values as well. There will be no more homelands, no
more national anthems, but only obscure brotherhoods and incantations. The whole earth will become septic, full of gangrene and
tentacular sects, bristling with fakirs and hallucinating prophets. On
the landings of the same building, people will be staking out their No
Man's Lands. Yes, it's good-bye to Their Majesties, good-bye to the
Presidents, good-bye to ballots and good-bye to electoral laws: people
will choose among the apprentice healers and their own divinities;
they will live on stupid rituals and be left to their suicidal exaltations.
Fundamentalism is already in the process of bringing faith back to
the worship of charlatans. The religions of the world will not be
able to hold out for long against the vertigo of diabolizations. The
churches will be replaced by the heretical temples. The mosques
will no longer dare to erect their minarets before the lodges of the
mutants. The third millennium wishes itself fundamentally mystical,
Llob. The apocalypse will blow your mind; you'll experience it as an
orgasm of enchantments.

I shake my head, groggy.

Da Achour is not one to favor gossip, but when he gives free
rein to his various moods, he's capable of raising the cassock of a
country priest.

He has not turned a hair, the old man; I see him smooth a
wrinkle on his temple. Once more his gaze is enveloped by foaming
breakers.

—I did not suspect the Mediterranean capable of inspiring

such depression, I reproach him. You used to be so hilarious—before. And to think that I came to recharge my batteries and get some fresh air in my lungs. What happened to that laughter-maker whose turns of phrase sent the Devil into a daze?

—Precisely. I am a bit like those puns which at first sight delight, and which upon reflection are meaningless.

—Take it easy, Da. What you're going through is the metabolism of your senility.

At last he turns around. His eyes still resemble the sea. Except that this morning no sailboat suggests evasion. He says: Do you know why the clowns paint their faces? The kids suppose it is for fun. An enormous red snout is more amusing than a nose. And the stars on their foreheads are less sad than the wrinkles. In reality, Llob, clowns color their faces to hide the telltale signs of their sorrow. It's their way of dissembling, of splitting their personality. A bit like the birds, who hide themselves to die. And who suspects the solitude of a clown in a festive circus? Nobody. And it's better that way. Only alone, in secret, does one see oneself as one really is.

He turns to face the sea again: For me, it's a whole island that detaches itself from my archipelago. There is tea in the thermos, Superintendent. It does not make a man happier, but it helps the digestion.

In the distance a steamer plays leapfrog with the waves. In the sky, boycotting our fields and our prayers, the gulls burst forth like white slogans. I sense I ought not to have disturbed an old man who 'knows' why the swell does not amuse the waves when it begins to toss and sway.

Chapter eight

The director recovers from our last interview as if from a bout of VD, his face as tortured as a rag. He is wearing a black suit, a gray tie and thick-lensed glasses to mask his ulterior motives. Bliss is beside him, falsely obsequious, almost pathetic in his status of polyglot in matters of servile flattery.

I storm into the office with a determined stride. I do not greet. I restrict myself to standing up, hands in pockets, as denuded of respect for the Republic as a Deputy in the Assembly. Bliss gives me a withering look of condemnation for my attitude. I ignore it. My mouth set assertively, I wait. The director pretends to be reading a report with that fake solemnity which corrupt judges affect. Assuredly he has spent hours fine-tuning his script. Now that I am here, he'll no doubt get his lines mixed up. In order to disconcert him still further, I tap my foot on the floor.

The director lowers his glasses a notch. His finger asks me to be patient, indicates an armchair. I think it advisable to take my time over easing into the seat, so as to get him faster into that bidet of a head—the slops he thrashes about in when I don't carry out one of his orders.

—Superintendent, I wish to…

—Let us understand each other well, Monsieur le Directeur, I cut him short. If it's to send us back the boomerang, I'm not in the mood.

His nostrils quiver, but he keeps his cool.

—Can't you see that Monsieur le Directeur wishes to be conciliatory, intervenes Bliss, contemplating his fingernails.

—You stay out of this, you dwarf, unless you want me to chuck you into the gutter and keep you there until the rats have finished sucking your bones.

Bliss recoils and is silent. His eyes narrow. This means he is the process of thinking, and when Bliss thinks, the Devil himself holds his breath.

The director is growing impatient, bids us to be sensible. After a long sigh he announces: Mourad Atti was handed over this morning to the Security Services for observation.

—I haven't finished with him.

—It's not serious. If he is connected in any way with our affair, the security boys have promised to let us know. I get up:

—Can I go now?

—Of course…

I smooth the front of my jacket down, take a few steps toward the door. His voice catches up with me:

—Superintendent…

I stop without turning round. The director descends from his throne and joins me. His bright red, delicately manicured hand rests on my shoulder before removing itself as if under the effect of an electric shock. He reaches the door before me, and caressing the handle, he simpers: You haven't anything special to do today…?

—That depends.

—If it's not too much trouble, try to pay a visit to our friend Ghoul.

—Not a hope. I broke my perch this morning.

—Meaning what?

—That it's over. Your friend would do better to hire a private detective.... For me, the asshole's affairs raise such a stench that I rarely see clearly. Find yourself another muckraker.

—You're not being serious, laments the boss.

—That's what I've been saying from the beginning.

❧

Lino is driving me home. He clutches the steering wheel and avoids looking at me. We have been driving for a good twenty minutes and it's deadly silent in the car. He knows that I've got a lot of people on my back and that troubles him.

—Those guys are bulldozers, he warns me.

—Don't care.

—What do you intend doing?

—Prepare my retirement. I'm no longer of an age that puts up with humiliations.

Lino admonishes me, wagging his index finger: It's not the time, Super. We're at war. They'll treat you as a deserter.

—Don't care.

—And your career, Super. Are you going to leave just when you're within an ace of becoming a divisional head?

It's at this point that I check him.

—The true career of a man, Lino, is his family. The one who has succeeded in life is the one who succeeds at home. The only fitting, worthy ambition is to be proud of one's home. The rest, all of it—promotion, dedication and vainglory—is nothing but ostentation, forward flight, diversion.

Lino remains silent. He drops me off at home and returns to the office, all tight-lipped.

❧

Misfortune never strikes singly. It doesn't have enough courage for that. It seems to need some supplementary tribulation to help it in its undermining work.

As I come into the house I stumble over two valises in the hallway. My eldest son is in the corridor, distressed but determined.

47

Seeing his mother in tears, I understand that he has decided to find somewhere else to bed down for good. For some time past, the idea of hoisting sail has been trotting around in his head. Algiers has become a real straitjacket for him. He no longer feels tenderness for his childhood neighborhood. His gaze flinches before me; he swallows:

—I'm sorry, Dad.

—It's not your fault, son.

He's a cop's son. In the fundamentalists' book he merits the same fate as his father. They slit the throats of quite a few kids simply because their parents were soldiers or policemen. I am almost relieved that he has decided on a change of scenery.

—Don't be too angry with me, Dad.

—It's not your fault, I tell you. Where are you heading for?

—Tamanrasset. I have friends there. I'll definitely find a job.

—I'm sure of it.

We gaze at one another in silence. Finally I open my arms to him and he comes to snuggle up against me. He has got much thinner, my eldest. Mina is awash in her tears. A mother is never anything but a mother; tears for her joy, and tears for her troubles. He picks up his valises. A terrible moment. A piece of my flesh is separating from me. I feel ill.

—Phone now and again.

—I promise.

He hugs his mother again, preparing to leave. The tide does indeed bring us some shells to furnish our memories with, but what it carries away is incalculable.

—Look after yourself, son.

He nods. A little smile, and the elevator snatches him from us. There is nothing worse to grow resigned to than a door that closes on a being who, the moment he leaves us, we already long for.

Chapter nine

It's quite by chance that Lino and I stumble on a commotion in the Oliviers district. No less than six police cars and two prison vans surround a villa under construction, the blue lamps rotating wildly and the windows shattered. Hidden under an engine hood, Inspector Serdj is perspiring, a bullhorn in one hand and in the other an obsolescent pistol. He is terribly relieved to see me drop from the sky.

—What's going on? I ask him, slipping in beside him.

—A band of terrorists attacked the post office in Bab Llyb. A citizen saw them go to ground here and alerted us.

—How many of them are there?

—Three. They've killed one hostage (he points to the body of a youngster at the foot of a cement mixer), and wounded one of my men.

I draw my pistol, adjust the sight to scout the terrain. A blast shatters the windscreen above my head. I ask:

—Have they been in there long?

—About an hour. They're refusing to surrender. There's a girl with them.

—Are they holding other people?

—The builder and his son.

—Weapons?

—Two Kalachnikov rifles and a shotgun.

Lieutenant Chater, from the Ninja section, crawls in our direction.

—Welcome to the action, Superintendent.

—How does it look?

—They're half-unconscious, drugged up to their eyeballs. I think we can get them. I've placed two marksmen over there, one on the roof and two more up there.

—You could have stationed another over there. I take him down a peg simply to assert my authority.

—Blind angle.

Smoke begins to billow out from one of the windows.

—They're starting to burn the post office loot, Chater explains.

—The dung! What are we going to use to reimburse the IMF with now?

I seize the bullhorn.

—You're wasting your time, Superintendent.

—It's so as to have nothing on my conscience afterward.

—Hey! *Taghout,** cries the girl. There is an old geezer and his bastard with us. Either you clear off or we'll first castrate them, then slice off their fingers, then their ears, then their toes, until there is nothing left to cut. If you are still around in five minutes, the first one will meet a very unpleasant end.

—They're not joking (Serdj is panic-stricken). In less than five minutes they are going to dismantle the first hostage.

—Still, we can't let them get away, protests Chater. They're itinerant executioners.

—Four minutes forty-five seconds. We'd better get moving lads.

I signal to Lino. He executes a stupendous slalom and comes and flattens himself against a wheel.

—Four minutes thirty seconds, panics Serdj.

—Shut up! We're not at NASA.

Small beads of sweat glisten on the Inspector's brow. His cheekbones quiver with tics. He bites his tongue without taking his eyes off his watch. I give Lino his briefing:

—There are two brave souls who are going to get wrecked in a few minutes if we don't go and get them right away. A father and son. According to Chater the three terrorists have been shooting barbiturates. We can finish them.

—I'm prepared, Chief, he cries, brandishing his 9mm.

—Cross yourself and stick close behind me.

I take a deep breath and charge onto the building site. The Kalachnikovs kick up a host of divots all around me. I dive into the cement gravel, crawl toward a container. Lino joins me, his expression distorted. To save face, he gives me an emphatic thumbs up.

—This is not the time to thumb a lift, I grunt.

A shot is fired from the roof. Someone screams inside the villa. A puppet appears, staggering, his jaw torn away. He collapses on the stairway and stiffens.

—Over here, I shout to the hostage.

The youngster refuses to listen to me. He is pinned against the ramp, transfixed by the corpse. Lino takes advantage of a fusillade to grab the boy by the arm and bring him into the shelter of the container. The exchanges of fire grow furious. The female terrorist comes into the open to machine gun us. The windscreens fly into fragments. The cops stand firm shoulder to shoulder in their dubious refuge. Chater fires. The woman lets go of her firearm, seeming not to know what's happening to her. Right between her eyebrows a bud begins to flower. She tries to cling to a girder, topples into space. Her siren's body bounces off the cement mixer before freezing in an indecent pose.

Lino and I pick this precise instant to begin our assault. We disappear into the hallway. The ground floor seems deserted. I go first, pistol to the fore. Lino follows close behind, his knees bent, and his rear so low that he resembles a female monkey urinating. The remaining terrorist is spewing out fire on the first floor.

I climb the steps cautiously, scraping my spine against the wall. Outside, Serdj and his team fire away on all cylinders to distract the terrorist. At last I can see him. He's a big, broad shouldered fellow, the type of target I'm fond of. He's using the constructor as a bulletproof shield.

Lino attempts a joke equal to the situation. I raise my pistol to my lips and he flattens himself. Chater's men resume spraying the building. The terrorist ripostes energetically. He doesn't hear me stationing myself behind him. With just time enough to notice that his goose is cooked, his head explodes like an enormous boil.

۞

Baya has lost her earring again. On all fours she searches under the desk, her posterior raised exaggeratedly. A yo-yo in the throat, Lino pretends indifference, one eye on the paper and the other on the moving rump. It is in this rather fascinating choreography that I come upon them.

—By dint of watching the peepshow, you're at risk of ending up a dishwasher in some execrable bar, I address the male of the species.

Baya gets up, confused, adjusts her skirt and vanishes like a shot.

To play the innocent, Lino wiggles his newspaper:

—They've killed the poet Jamal Armad!

—I know about it.

—For Heaven's sakes! He was only twenty-five.

I hang up my coat on a nail, find that it has the air of a flag at half-mast, so go and lay it on the back of my chair.

—What a waste! Why the devil do they target intellectuals like that, Super?

—It's not something new Lino. It's an old story. Traditionally, in our secular lack of culture, the lettered one has always been the outsider, the foreigner or the conqueror. We have deeply resented this difference. We have become viscerally allergic to intellectuals. And with us, of course, as is always the case—we might be able to forgive the crime, but never the difference.

Lino pushes his glasses away and protests:

—Lack of culture? Why do you say lack of culture?

—It's on account of an unfortunate slip of the tongue. Very long ago our ancestor wished to write a book. Since he could not reflect on an empty stomach, the tribe prepared a fantastic feast for him, and he stuffed himself with so much food that the moment he sat down to attack the manuscript, he noticed that what he really wanted to do was to take a siesta. The problem was that he was afraid that the moment he woke up his muse would desert him. A real dilemma. Then Saint Ziri, the father of us all, appeared to him. He asked him what was the matter. Our ancestor explained to him that at one and the same time he had an insurmountable desire to sleep and an immeasurable need to write his memoirs. Saint Ziri, who had been a great patron of the letters when alive, had this very unfortunate slip of the tongue. Instead of saying to him *redige*, 'write,' he said to him: *digere*, 'digest'. And since then, we have not stopped digesting.

—My grandpa never told me anything like that.

—That's because he couldn't speak with his mouth full.... Where are we with the three terrorists from yesterday?

—It's Serdj who's dealing with it.

—Anyone else would surprise me.

Serdj's office is adjacent to the toilets at the end of the corridor; there hangs over it an unbearable mix of tobacco fumes and stench. One might imagine oneself in the laboratory of a hallucinating scientist. The place is awash with waste paper, the cigar butts are decomposing on the ground, the cupboards open their arms, the drawers put out their tongues...

Serdj is indispensable to this place. He does not know how to turn down a request. The people he studied with are all now either superintendents or high officials, while he limps along benignly in his twelfth year as a low-level inspector. Because he is submissive and indispensable, they refuse to allow him to benefit from training or a grant, those two promotional criteria exclusively reserved for those with pull, or for undesirables they wish to be rid of. I settle myself on a chair and cross my legs.

—Have they identified the terrorists?

—The girl is not known to us. Her fingerprints told us nothing.

53

As for the redheaded guy, he's Daho Lamine, thirty-one years old; a bachelor. His father is so loaded with dough that he has his socks made to measure.

—And the other one?

—Brahim Boudar, thirty-seven. Married. Divorced. No profession. Five years in prison for molesting a minor. Two years for assault and battery. Nine months for using drugs. Wounded and arrested in September 1993. Escaped from Sidi Ghiles in '94.

—That's all?

—Brahim Boudar was one of the main architects of October 1988. He set the Galeries Algeriennes at Kouba, the El Fellah markets at Cheraga, and Boufarik on fire.

—Was he a little Brother at that time?

—Bouncer in a cabaret, the Limbes Rouges.

—Interesting.

—One more detail: arrested in '88, his right-hand man at the time was a certain Mourad Atti.

Lino bangs on the table:

—I knew we hadn't finished with that faggot.

With a gesture from my index finger, I advise him to calm down; then get up, my eyebrows lowered:

—I want Mourad Atti in my office at 3 PM on the dot.

Serdj pulls a face: There's just one problem, boss. I contacted the boys at Obs. They formally assured me that that individual never set foot in their place.

—And the discharge?

—From the can. The Obs doesn't recall having authorized anyone with transferring the suspect. The two types who turned up were phonies. The director was tricked...

—So where is he, then?

۲€

—There he is, Superintendent, says a policeman, guiding me over the mounds of a municipal rubbish dump.

Mourad Atti is lying in the midst of a pile of rubbish. Flat on his stomach. The back of his head blown away by the impact from a high caliber rifle. A cloud of flies hover around his brain.

—A tramp reported him, added the policeman, pressing a handkerchief hard against his face.

I crouch in front of the corpse. He has handcuffs on his wrists and his feet have been bound with wire. His big, tortured eyes seem to be telling me something in confidence. The gendarme warns me:

—Don't touch him. He's booby-trapped.

❧

Two days later, as I'm trying to see what's making the bay of Algiers sullen by rubbing my nose against my office window, there's a phone call from Anissa, the inflatable doll at the Cinq Etoiles.

—I have heard that you are invited to Madame Fa Lankabout's, Superintendent.

—Correct. But I am planning on not going there because of my ulcer. If you haven't a cavalier, I can arrange it. I have a lieutenant who adores riding.

The little one's breathing becomes more rapid.

—I have to hang up, she gasps in a fissured voice. Let's meet at Fa's, Monsieur Llob. I've got some things to tell you.

—Can't you save me the hassle and tell me now?

—I can't. See you this evening.

She hangs up. With a gesture of his hand Lino asks me what's going on.

—A lady is giving a reception.

—When?

—This evening.

—You're lucky, Super.

—If you want, I'll invite you along too.

He drops the pencil he was gnawing at.

—It's not right to tease me, Super. It's not fair.

—Cross my heart.

—For real? You're inviting me to a reception, with girls and all?

55

—If I were you I'd rush out and get a pack of condoms.

He can't believe his luck. My lieutenant is so delighted that he almost leaps to the ceiling. Like the Pope presented with a Christmas present.

Chapter ten

When a gallant rendezvous with the opposite sex is involved Lino doesn't hesitate to dynamite his piggy bank. This time he must have dipped into his mother's savings. He is shining like a new *sou*: cherry jacket, Italian shoes, and British-style tie; hair plastered down with brilliantine. A revolution. As I draw up to the sidewalk, he takes care to scrupulously wipe the seat before climbing into my old jalopy.

—What incense have you doused yourself with? I say to him as we move off.

—Ah! You must have recovered from your cold, chief. It's a Parisian perfume.

—Experimental?

—Not at all, he retorts indignantly. There's a brand name and all.

I overtake a truck and remark:

—You must have taken the wrong bottle, dear. Seeing that mosquito in a coma on the dashboard, it was probably an insecticide that you picked up.

Lino guffaws as he studies my own attire—the dowdy garb of an incorruptible officer of the law.

—Look Chief, go right ahead and admit you're jealous of how I'm turned out!

We arrive at Madame Fa Lankabout's a little after nightfall. Lino refuses to believe that such splendor can exist in a war-torn country. Truth to tell, I have invited him with the express purpose of waking him up, and to dispel, once and for all, those slogans and idiotic notions about probity and transparency that got crammed into his skull.

Madame Fa looks superb. Her makeup girls have surpassed themselves. Swathed in a jewel-encrusted gown, she brings to mind cooked meat wrapped in cellophane. She is so courted that she has only a fleeting smile for me. Meanwhile Lino, literally surrounded by females in rut, displays the enthusiasm of a canine—he wags his tail. He casts a glance at the decolletés of some, at the behinds of others, and he gulps so hard as to almost dislocate his Adam's apple.

—Beautiful stable! Do you think I have a chance of saddling one of those mares, Super? I've been abstaining for such a long time that I'm beginning to have a soft gherkin where my dick should be.

—Help yourself—just watch out for the heavy petticoats.

—Of what?

—Of the transvestites, idiot.

He raises his eyebrows and admits without shame: I'm not so demanding, you know.

I try to locate the young features of Anissa in the jigsaw of charm. She isn't there. On rounding a discreet crush we are accosted by two magnificent creatures with just enough covering their flesh to avoid having the Morals Police out in force. The redhead wiggles like a meat fly larva, her pupils afire with passion. The other is a brunette, thin and openly flaunting the nature of her appetites. Lino surprises himself by slobbering on two levels.

—Aren't you in the movies? the brunette meows at him in the hollow of his shoulder.

—It's possible, lies the lieutenant.

—It's just that you resemble Woody Allen! clucks the red-head.

—Personally, I'd rather see him in Idir, I say.

—Why?

—Well, obviously, because he's circumcised....

The two kittens are shocked. They take the bespectacled one by the arm and drag him toward the buffet.

—Who is that dummy? Is he with you?

—Not at all, Lino treacherously denies. He must be some vagrant that Madame Fa has brought along to replenish the chests of her charitable association.

Alone, I'm now at leisure to take an interest in the surrounding fauna. The Lankabout dwelling is a veritable Olympus swarming with common garden gods and *houris.** The hostess has mobilized close to a regiment of domestics to pamper her crowd. A glass of orangeade in my hand, I decide to take stock of the guests. It's practically the same crowd as at Ghoul Malek's son-in-law's, a collection of social-climbing snobs to make you swallow your slippers.... Hey! Relax Llob! There's nothing better than a suppository to restore your drive. I recognize Rachid Lagoune, the president of the late "SOS Ostracisme", a populist movement against exclusion in general and the marginalization of the elite in particular. A tough outsider, once. He was present at all the meetings, a microphone between his teeth, insolently defying the hirelings of the regime. Persistent occupant of all the State penitentiary establishments, he was well on the way to becoming a myth. I am astounded to find him around here.

Now, with a glass straw up his nostril, he's having a whale of a time. There's a ring in his ear, he has grown a ponytail and his bow tie raises his chin to a considerable height, *he*—defender of the proletariat!

—I see you've turned coat, I whisper to him.

Irritated by my indelicacy, he apparently casts around in his mind to recall which kennel he could have come across a louse of my species.

—Better, he retorts, I've got myself a new one.

—Don't you fight for the good causes any longer?

—All causes are good, provided there is intoxication there. Do we know each other?

—Don't think so. I used to know a Rashid Lagoune once. He was a homo, that one.

He measures me from head to toe and spits out:

—Good evening, Monsieur, may I have the pleasure of never seeing you again.

A little further on I am intercepted by Sid Lankabout, the scribbler of the old regime. God, how I detest him! No more talent than a slipper has a heel. On the other hand, an unequaled opportunist. He started out as a Communist in the days when Marxism meant reading like a maniac. Then he was a surrealist when cybernetic literature forced the admiration of the dunces, so Lankabout devoted himself principally to the drafting of stereotyped speeches while forging some first-rate contacts for himself among the dinosaurs of Algerian socialism. He even went to teach in a *lyceé*, so as to make the youth disgusted with reading. Morbid Arabist, he bears responsibility for the inquisition of the francophones and the majority of the student conflicts recorded in the universities. And nowadays, when intellectuals are being executed without prior warning, he is bizarrely one of the rare writers to do his shopping in the full light of day without glancing to the right or to the left.

As is frequently the case in the thieves' cauldron that is literature, where rivalries are highly subjective and cordiality is based on calculating pettiness and booby-trapped bouquets, the Lankabout-Llob relationship has always been reptilian, that is to say simultaneously hushed and venomous: he consigning my art to the status of minor genre, and I brutally contesting his renown as the Don Quixote '*des arts et des letters*,' of perjuries and debtor's bills. So it is in the shadow of this hinterland of enmities that we shake hands.

—What's stopping you from handing in your badge, Llob? A whole era has gone by without a cop being put out to pasture. What's more, the vocation of novelist is incompatible with the profession of annoying people.

—A whole era has gone by without putting a writer out to

pasture, either. Why not begin by hanging up your own pen, Monsieur Lankabout?

He gazes into his glass as if expecting to find a subject there to plagiarize. He speaks out of the corner of his mouth:

—It seems that you are in the process of giving birth to a third tome?

—This time I'm writing about anti-matter.

—Interesting, I didn't know you were an alchemist. Does anti-matter really exist?

—Fundamentalism is its most active manifestation.

—What do you reproach it with, you who are fundamentally pious, Monsieur Llob?

—I blame it for its new, insidious meaning.

—I see. Rather a risky thesis, don't you think?

—It's to compensate for my lack of talent.

He shakes his head:

—Hmm! One way or another to force the hand of glory. One *fatwa* and you'll be immediately propelled to winning the Goncourt literary prize. There are lots of hacks for whom it's worked.

—The proof is before me.

—Perhaps, but my risks were minimal. I must pay tribute to your damned courage.

—What do you know about courage, Monsieur Lankabout?

—I know that it is a crudely false maneuver.

He twists his mouth into a malevolent grimace, shakes his glass, raises it to his lips but does not drink. For a long moment, his hypocritical eyes distill their venom into mine.

—If only you could manipulate your pen with as great an ease as your tongue, Superintendent. It has been a real pain to have run into you, Ali Baba.

—Same here, Ali Gator.

≱€

My watch reminds me that it's already a good two hours that Anissa has had me hanging around. Haj Garne arrived ten minutes ago. Finding my presence unbearable, he has had to apologize to the master of the house—who proved singularly accommodating—and took off again, letting it be understood that it was sufficient to have one overstuffed glutton farting at a table to spoil the whole banquet.

Madame Fa finds a moment to escape the attentions of her gigolos. She corners me and makes me feel that I am within an inch of dethroning Rabelais. Her hand does not stop inquiring into the robustness of my abdominal muscles. It is true that she has the mania of punctuating her remarks with insistent pokings, as is the case with those who don't manage to make themselves understood on essentials, but she overdoes it somewhat. A waste of effort. Then she realizes that I shall not be figuring at her sabbatical hit parade list and abandons the attempt.

Just as I am taking a bite, I spot Ghoul Malek's albino in the back room, solidly camped on his heels, resembling a eunuch awaiting a snapping of the fingers. Just time to peck at the buffet and return, and he has vanished.

For his part, Lino has not shown any signs of life since climbing upstairs in the company of the two mice. Going to find him, a door that is ajar elicits my attention. A rapid glance confirms that Anissa's delay is not due to some mechanical breakdown. The little one is there, flat on the Lankabouts' bed, her dress hoisted above her thighs, her panties around her calves.

Her killer must have suffocated her against the pillow while he was having sex with her.

Chapter eleven

I collect Serdj and we go over Anissa's apartment at the Cinq Etoiles with a fine toothcomb. Save for the marks of a camera behind the knick-knacks—which suggest that the amorous frolics of the girl were duly inventoried—absolutely nothing. No intimate jottings, no phone notebook, nor any kind of diary. The jewels were undisturbed, but the family photographs had disappeared.

We look under the carpet, scrape the backs of drawers in search of an incriminating cufflink or nail clipping; not a sausage. So it's one of two things: either Anissa carried a computer program in her head or else someone got there before us.

I catch the floor attendant spying on us through the keyhole. Caught flagrantly in the act, he agrees to cooperate. In his way; he does not recall whether Anissa had left alone or in company the day she was killed, swears on his mother's head that he had taken her to be the daughter of a dowered widow, and that he knew absolutely nothing about what she got up to.

The rest of the staff comes from the same mould. Accustomed to large tips, they have got into the habit of recovering their memory only in relation to the largesse of people suffering from nostalgia. The hotel director just spreads his arms wide. He cannot even recall the little one. For him, a client is a work tool, making the business run just like a young bellboy or an elevator cable. It's a room number, a bill for the accounts department. How the client dresses, what machinations he gets up to in the privacy of his room—these are of no concern to the management.

Having been denied access to the Limbes Rouges, I had a brainwave. I charged Lino with ferreting around in those parts. One never knows: an indiscretion might just not fall on deaf ears. Lino returned empty handed, his eye and his pocket revolted. This didn't cause me too much distress. Lino would find the ocean dry if called upon to display his prowess as a water diviner.

Serdj spends the rest of the day consulting his archives. I simmer in my stall, finger in nose; ignoring the heroics of a cockroach engaged in combat with my shoelaces. Through the window the sun spies on me lopsidedly. In the distance on his hill, draped in a shroud of spray, the colossus of Maqam* hesitates about whether he should throw himself into the sea. It reminds me of the brave souls of this world who, failing to admit their incompetence, make out they are reflecting on weighty matters, whereas truly they are in the throes of dozing off. I pretend to be preoccupied. A chief, even when he is snoring his head off, does not sleep; he ruminates, he transcends, he is ever vigilant. Just as I begin to sink into the arms of Morpheus, Serdj comes to wreck my reveries, a crumpled photo in his hand:

—Maybe this will help.

In the photo, Anissa is on Haj Garne's arm during a reception. She is smiling from ear to ear, radiating happiness. In the background I recognize the arid features of the Madame of the Limbes and close behind her, Mourad Atti.

—How does this help us? I ask in exasperation.

Serdj skirts round my desk to lean over my shoulder.

—It was taken on January 29.

—What of it?

My slowness on the uptake disconcerts him: Anissa's real name was Soria Atti. Mourad was her cousin.

I raise my hand to my mouth to stifle a yawn. Serdj sponges

himself with a handkerchief. He notes how unmotivated I am, and doesn't know whether to leave his report for later or to continue. I encourage him.

—Do go on...

—Well, on the night between January 29 and 30, a certain Abbas Laouer suffered a heart attack while undergoing exquisite sexual torture in one of the rooms of the cabaret. His kinetic therapist was Anissa.

—Listen, you're starting to make me dizzy with all this beating around the bush. Get to the point, there's a good man. Aim straight for the goal, it's the shortest way.

The schizophrenia of a superior not being an excuse for mutiny. Serdj takes my strictures in good spirit and explains.

—Abbas Laouer was the director of the National Bank. He had serious problems. His coffers were showing a deficit of 120 million dollars.

Now I recall how this death made headlines in all the papers. Some of them even went so far as to advance the thesis of a murder coverup. I had only vaguely got wind of the affair at the time. Stories of the embezzlement of public funds are common currency with us. From the famous *soudouq al-tadamoun* ('solidarity fund') created the day after Independence, to the remarkable hospital benefit telethon, via the scandalous affair of the twenty-six billion, it has become a regular news item by dint of its extreme banality. Now my lassitude prompts Serdj to take a short cut. With his ink-stained finger he taps the face of Mourad Atti.

—The little girl surely had an inkling regarding her cousin's death. Perhaps she felt herself threatened as well or else she simply lost control. This is the third time that the Limbes card has hit us in the eye. In my opinion we ought to have a little chat with Superintendent Dine*. He was the one investigating the death of Abbas Laouer.

—Dine is in the asylum.

—He left the asylum a month ago. I've checked. In any case, we have no choice.

Dine shows me into his pitiable apartment in the cheap housing project; much more a slum than anything else. He has aged terribly. His corpulence has vanished, his joviality as well. Disheveled, his gaze dull, one could collect rainwater in his sunken cheeks. He is a man undone, emptied out, who totters and sniffles; an insubstantial creature in the feeble light of the room.

Our meeting has the chill of confrontation. He proffers neither handshake nor smile; I am given the sense that I'm disturbing a certain order. Sitting down opposite him, I find myself unable to summon the strength to inquire how he is. On the table that separates us, there's a bottle of alcohol catching cold in its base, next to an ashtray as full as an urn. Around us it's chaos: mattress on the floor, slippers upturned, dirty plates, dust, a bad odor.

Dine first rolls up his pajama trouser leg to scratch his calf. His leg has an unhealthy whiteness. Then, gropingly, he picks up a packet of cigarettes from the floor.

—I see that you've recovered your puffer-train enthusiasm.

—It's a change for me from the breath of smokers. Sorry, I can't offer you any coffee.

—Never mind. Your youngsters aren't here?

—I don't like seeing them wandering about within reach of my hangovers. I sent them to Oran.

I nod:

—Yes, aren't we *all* passing through zones of turbulence.

He doesn't notice the stressed word. In a drink-befuddled voice he repeats:

—Zones of turbulence.

He sinks back in his worn armchair, blowing elaborate smoke rings. Fleetingly, an idiotic smile flowers under his mustache; then he suddenly frowns, as if just noticing my presence.

—Why have you come, Llob?

—Are you in a hurry for me to leave?

—One can hide nothing from you.

I rise, stand in front of the window. Outside, Algiers loses interest in the Mediterranean. Dismembered on its hills it gazes at the sun like some broken-down yard, an inaccessible grain of maize. Several

ships are anchored at sea, taciturn and suspicious. The country's shores
are not what they once were. Down below, in the block's scooped out
courtyard, two urchins are squinting into the driving mirror of my
Zastava. A third clambers onto the car and slides on the hood with
a loud burst of laughter.

—Why have you come?

I turn round. Dine lights another cigarette from the butt of
the preceding one. His hands are feverish; he reminds me of a granny
inserting her dentures bit by bit.

—It's to do with the Limbes.

—I am no longer involved.

—But I am.

He contemplates his cigarette, loses himself for a moment in
his obsessions.

—It's a shooting range, Llob. There are too many snipers.

—Is that why you left?

—I'm fifty-two-years-old, I have eight mouths to feed, and
not a sou put aside.

—Were you threatened?

He throws back his head with a sickly laugh.

—They don't threaten the unimportant ones. They send
them two young rascals younger than their own kids and the affair
is shelved.

—Who's 'they'?

—That is your problem. I have resigned. I rise when I wish,
sleep when I feel like it, and even if I don't always put my nose out
of doors, I have the consolation of not mistaking my shadow for a
terrorist.

He crushes his cigarette butt aggressively in the ashtray. His
hands ball into fists, fall onto his knees. For a few minutes I am
vouchsafed several curious, wordless gestures. Then he recovers a trace
of his former lucidity, unwinds.

—Those people have no more scruples than a stone crusher,
he says, as if to himself. Wherever you forget a finger, wherever you
let your feet drag, you won't even have the time to realize the gravity
of your carelessness. You will find yourself in a piteous state. Their

lackeys are everywhere; in the administration, among your colleagues, in your cupboard. They will crush you like a fly.

He rubs his index finger against his thumb in a mystical gesture.

—Just like that, with two fingers. And after that you are no longer there. Erased. You must be asking yourself whether I would not have done better to have remained a little longer among the crazies. Well, you are right. One has to be fucked in the head to dare to disturb the shit of gods.

He searches around him, dazed, a liquid pearl at the end of his nose. His pack of cigarettes is empty. He crumples it with a menacing clench, chucks it against the wall. The cop I once took so much pride in now only stirs a kind of troubling compassion in me.

To ease the situation, I turn back toward the window. The neighborhood hides itself behind its sordid buildings, ashamed and scared at the same time. The three urchins have moved on to another car.

—Haven't you got any of the file lying around?

—You wouldn't get a page of it. If you insist on risking your old idiot skin, it will be without my blessing.

—I have names on my desk. I have to establish the link between them.

—Don't exhaust yourself. I'm no longer in the game. Now buzz off. It's time for my pills.

I don't insist. He catches up with me on the landing.

—There are too many base intrigues, Llob. You haven't got the power. The Limbes is a minefield. Those people leave nothing to chance. They never retreat or hesitate, and they don't make any concessions. Think it over; you really don't have to do it. Think it over carefully. There are matters one deals with, and there are those one avoids like the plague.

—I do my job. If I chance to skid to the right in the middle of a journey—well, those are the risks of the profession.

He threatens me with a trembling finger:

—Don't say I haven't warned you!

—Quit smoking, Dine. Above all, quit drinking.

Chapter twelve

The comedian Ait Meziane has just been assassinated. He was dropping his daughter off at college when two armed individuals fired three bullets into the back of his neck. There is interference on the line, and the speaker adds something that I do not catch.

The news strikes me like a whiplash. I remain doubled over my shoelaces, incapable of completing getting dressed.

Flashes of recollections race through my thorn-covered head: a school playground where, as a child, the victim was initiated into clowning; a corner of the classroom where the teacher placed a paper crown topped by two ass' ears on his head; the boards of a rudimentary stage upon which he prepared to win the hearts of people, then the auditorium of the Central Theater where he had come to tear at mine.

—Shit!

Mina turns down the radio. She knows how much Ait meant to me. Her eyes grow misty. She leans back against the wall and clenches her fist.

Without uttering a word I finish tying my laces, get up, slip on my jacket and go into the kitchen. Without uttering a word, I put two lumps of sugar in my coffee and jam on my slice of bread, and eat breakfast while contemplating a scratch mark on the windowpane. Three blasts of the hooter announce Lino's arrival.

Without uttering a word I wipe my mouth on a rag and reach the landing, forgetting to close the door behind me.

The sun flushes out night's final pockets of resistance entrenched deep in the big gateways. Its galvanized light ricochets off the window panes, bursts on the bodywork of cars, pours forth in a multitude of tiny lights on the dew-lubricated pavements, and not a single spark manages to light up the eyes of the passersby.

People pass one another in an inaudible rustling, their minds elsewhere, with the steps of sleepwalkers. Something in their gait betrays a profound resignation. Theirs is the attitude of those who are unhappy with the Messiah; theirs is the silence of those who no longer get on with each other.

Lino opens the car door for me. He says nothing, not even a desultory "hello." He knows that I *know*. Without uttering a word we make our way through the fog. At the office Serdj informs me that one of the two assassins of Ait Meziane has been apprehended. Immediately I imagine myself eating him alive. Entering the cell where he is being held, I am instantly deflated.

He is there, crouching in a corner, ashen-faced and shivering with cold. An adolescent barely taller than a rifle. Visibly out of his depth with the way things have turned out. Like a trapped bird his gaze travels in all directions without meeting mine. He trembles, his hands between his thighs, his lips like two viscous, elastic slugs. I immediately understand that with him as a guide we are not ready to leave the inn.

He begins with unintelligible denials. After half an hour he weakens; he works as an apprentice mechanic at the Place de la Gare. In the beginning, 'they' entrusted him with minor stuff; small errands here, a message there. Afterward they entrusted him with raising the alarm the moment a local 'despot' came home. He had to hang his jacket on the lintel of the door.

—It's Didi who shoots. I finger the target for him and keep a lookout. After the hit, I hide the weapon in the workshop. Someone comes to retrieve it in the evening.

He had been recruited the day after a police raid in town, five months previously. He was coming back from the baths. Some cops threw him into a police van. Three hours at the station. He wasn't brutalized but they took his family details and his address, etc. For Didi this meant the black list. "You're cooked!" Didi had shouted at him. "One day when they don't have anyone to sink their teeth into, it's you they'll come and get!"

—I didn't know that Didi would betray me, he whines. Didi promised to look after me. He would slip me some pennies and take me to the stadium. He said that we were brothers and that God was blessing what we did. He gave me sacks to look after at home. Then a revolver. Then all at once the target was a neighbor, someone who'd once been working for TV.

—How many assassinations did you take part in?

—Only three, I swear it. Not one more. It was Didi who did the shooting. I don't even know how to load a gun.

—Who was the second victim?

—Jamal Armad. Didi said a lot of bad things about him. He said that he was Satan, that he wrote obscenities and that he was perverting the youth.

—Where is Didi?

—I don't know. He never told me where he lived. When he has a job for me, he stands in front of the workshop. I meet him in a café, two hundred meters away. He explains what's involved and fixes the rendezvous with me. Afterward, he goes in one direction and I go in another.

In the afternoon Serdj brings me an identikit picture.

—You remember the Bonzo with the pumped up muscles who blocked the entrance to the Limbes Rouges? Well, that's him, that's Didi.

࿐

The neon sign of the Limbes Rouges daubs the road with a violent array of blood-tinted streaks. Intermittently, the nightclub door slides open on a fanfare of music, devoured instantly by the wind. A drizzle weeps for the fine evenings of yesteryear and the trees tear out their tresses in melodramatic hysteria. The bands of buddies who laughed under the stars, the insomniac streets and the discourse of drunks debating their own hallucinations—all of them have vanished.

Now the rue des Lauriers-roses is no more than a lake of absence and neglect that the cabaret haunts like a malevolent island. Barely a few months ago, kiosks lined the esplanade all the way to the heart of the market. Night owls strolled peacefully, counting the port lights. There were ham actors who regaled one another with tales of their adventures, who dreamed of dream countries. It was not exactly a paradise, but it was less depressing than the hell that followed. This evening the rue des Lauriers-roses is champing at the bit. Its buildings are under police surveillance. No more kebab vendors, no more gigolos in search of gilded adultery. People lock themselves indoors and hold their breath; even the sound of a neighbor's dish breaking quickly has the entire neighborhood in a panic.

From time to time, between two police patrols, a phantom vehicle hisses softly on the waterlogged roadway, stops in front of the nightclub. The cabaret door closes, and the universe is rapidly abandoned to the lamentations of the rain and the contortions of the trees.

We are parked in an angle of the street, underneath a one-eyed standard lamp. We smoke our cigarettes. Sitting in the old crate with its steamed-up windows, Lino reproaches the hands on his watch for failing to make progress. For him, to be stuck inside a fetid old jalopy, cramped on a decaying car seat waiting for the little bird to emerge, is a punishment. He holds it against me for having mobilized him during a curfew and considers himself to be arbitrarily over-exploited. Lino is short-circuiting himself quite unnecessarily: when I get an idea screwed into my head, a pair of pliers would break its teeth on it.

The little bird comes out about one AM; she's a young girl of about twenty, lovely as a smile, doe-eyed, and svelte as a smoke spiral. She looks like she could belly dance better than a cobra.

We let her coil herself into her Renault and drive along by the port. Once past a police barrier we cross a downtown neighborhood with the air of an Indian cemetery, bypass a part of Bab el Oued where the simple folk fornicate ardently to keep themselves warm, and climb the sinuous road which leads to the city heights. Without warning the hovels vanish and we burst upon a little Eden bedecked with opulent villas, Swiss chalets and hanging gardens. Lino, who was reared in the vicinity of a rubbish dump, cannot believe his eyes. He pivots his neck so much he risks snagging his vertebrae, over-whelmed, subdued by the sumptuous dwellings which have chosen to deploy their insouciance not two steps from the misery of the ghettos.

—Hell! Just take a peek at those fortresses, Super. I hope you've obtained a visa for us. Where the heck are we? I reckon you put your foot down too hard on the accelerator. We've gone through the sound barrier...

I say nothing. I try to concentrate on the Renault, so as not to look.

Lino, quite frankly, has got a drawbridge stuck in his mouth. Poor fellow! He hasn't yet realized that in his beloved country every-one is busily engaged in building palaces for their offspring and no one thinks of building a homeland for them. The Renault mounts the pavement, glides into a garage and extinguishes its lights. I con-fide to Lino: Now that we know where Didi's little friend lives, I am charging you with keeping a twenty-four hour round-the-clock surveillance on the house.

His drawbridge is lowered and his pointed chin falls onto his chest.

I offer him some crumbs of comfort:

—Well, it'll give you a change from the ugliness of your own hovel....

❧

Lino spent a week ferreting around the dancer without seeing so much as a trace of Didi. Meanwhile, he recognized a drug dealer who visited the girl on two occasions. The first time on the day after the assassination of Ait Meziane; the second, in a Mercedes with an albino at the wheel.

After a whole string of risky maneuvers we managed to locate the dealer's den.

Lino, Serdj, Chater and I decided to pay him a small courtesy call. Serdj and Chater would give us cover from a café, facing a cul de sac. The bespectacled one and I creep along, ending up in the yard of an abandoned warehouse. Some youngsters are there, balancing on barrels and vying with each other to see who can piss farthest. The remains of a tractor rust in a corner, covered in dust and excreta. We disappear inside the hangar. Lino almost disfigures himself on a step.

—That's my hand under your shoe, groans a tramp, from beneath a pile of rags.

We beg his pardon and advance toward a putrefying trash heap. A small door concealed beneath a metal staircase vomits us out onto a passage so narrow that we have to advance in single file. Down below a slum ruminates upon its misfortune. Two children of tender age play with a gas bottle under the absent-minded gaze of an ancient man. A skylight comes to our rescue and leads us onto a landing that I would not even wish on my Algerian publisher. No guard railing, no lighting, just scooped out steps suspended in the black, ready to hurl you into the void.

The door that interests us seems to be gathering moss at the end of the corridor. To the left we can hear a baby wailing. I draw my rod and kick in the lock.

—Police!

A crash of a table, two curses, and a gun spits in our direction.

I burst in first, firing at random. A ragged curtain bids us farewell. The dealer takes off over the rooftops. He is not alone. A clubfoot hops along behind him, his behind wholly in front of him.

—Police! No one move!

A group of women interrupt the hanging up of their laundry and fly in all directions, screeching. The clubfoot catches his foot in a bucket, falls and lets off a volley of lead at us. Lino ripostes and hits him in the shoulder.

The dealer returns to give his friend a hand, vacillates before our advance, and weighs the pros and cons. Deciding, he burns the brains of the clubfoot and darts away through a laundryroom.

—Take the staircase, I shout to Lino.

The lieutenant disappears.

Beyond the laundry room there is another terrace. An elevator cage plunges down into a horrific building. Women scream behind their doors. I descend into hell, weak at the knees.

—Give me back my child, sobs a mother. He's sick. Leave him alone.

The dealer is backed into a dead end, with a kid as a human shield. Lino moves heaven and earth to hold the mother back.

—Let the little one go, I say to the dealer.

—It's you who are going to take your fucking butt out of here. His eyes gleam with a strange jubilation.

—You will have him on your conscience, he warns me. Me, I have nothing to lose. One move, and the cherub's face won't be a pleasant sight.

And he sniggers.

I know this type of crackpot. If I lower my gun he will shoot at me and get away with the kid. If I keep my gun trained on him, I gain time for reflection. Lino attempts a diversion. The dealer corrects him with a burst of crossfire.

—Don't move, you pile of crap!

—If you touch one hair of that kid, I swear I'll cut you into little pieces.

He furiously musses the urchin's hair, and sneers: you've lost, you motherfucker. You are going to fast for three days non-stop. In the meantime stand on the side and drop your toy.

Behind him Serdj's head sticks up over a wall.

—Okay, I say gently extending my arm. Let the little one go—

—Your plaything on the ground, and make it snappy.

Serdj signals to me to agree. My stomach twists into knots. Itchy sweat cascades down my back. The dealer continues to snigger, and it is his cold and cynical smile that scares me.

—Move it, fucking cop.

My piece falls to the ground. I don't know what happened. Like in a dream, I see the dealer push the kid toward Lino to protect his flank, and lift the cannon in my direction. A shot…any moment now I expect to collapse. The dealer doesn't flinch. He sniggers, sniggers, then his teeth redden, and a filament of blood begins to trickle from the corners of his mouth. He pivots in slow motion and crashes to the ground.

Serdj leaps down from the wall and kicks away the dealer's piece before bending over him.

—He's still breathing. Get an ambulance—fast!

※

The dealer is a certain Slimane Abbou. Serdj's bullet passed through a lung without causing too much damage. According to the doctor, he will have to remain under observation. I promised him I'd keep an eye on Abbou. A search of his place enabled us to lay our hands on a fax, two hunting rifles with sawn-off barrels, munitions, bomb-making gear, manuals for the handling of explosives, tracts signed by Abou Kalybse and a list containing the names of twenty-three intellectuals, eight of which have been marked with a cross, including the poet Jamal Armad, Sissane Miloud from the TV and the performer Ait Meziane. Either Abou Kalybse detests my style or else he doesn't read detective novels, because I haven't been listed for his festival.

Chapter thirteen

Omar Malkom, aka Iks, owns an electrical goods store in a peaceful neighborhood. His store radiates onto the pavement, pleasantly decorated, with an immense bay window and a small door that chimes when pushed. He's busy scribbling in a register, a pile of receipts on the side. Serdj closes the door, turns the 'open' notice to 'closed' to ensure that no one disturb us, and crosses his arms. I announce myself: How much is the fridge?

Omar, raising his hand to ask that his concentration not be disturbed, punches on a calculator and checks his index cards, his tongue hanging out in the manner of a schoolchild. He is a Black of a respectable size, with fists capable of making an ass swallow its dentures. He wears a banker's three-piece suit, a fob watch on a golden chain and Ray Ban fantasy specs. His cranium is severely shorn at the temples with just a small square of phosphorescent green hair above the forehead.

—Are your accounts in order, punk?

He lays down his pen, reluctantly.

—Which fridge?

I show him my 'taghout' cop card.

—This company does not accept that type of credit card. Here, one pays cash in hand.

—Nah, that's just too bad…you've got me all stressed out.

He lifts an embarrassed hand to his brow:

—Cops—that's all we need. You'll bring bad luck to my business. Do they know you in these parts? If that's the case, I shall have to move away.

—There's no hurry, Serdj reassures him.

Iks extricates himself from his counter, and waddling, goes to lower the blinds.

—Are you here to arrest me or to gossip?

—That rather depends on you.

He laughs mirthlessly:

—Tsst! I've been vaccinated.

—A revaccination would not be ill advised.

He scrutinizes me once again, waggles his tail end and returns to behind his barricade. Judging by his unbridled casualness, he must surely be a Spike Lee fan.

—Listen, brother, I'm on the level. My books are as straight as the Penal Code.

—Mourad Atti, he was your mate.

Not a fiber of panic on his ebony face. Calmly he strokes his calculator. After a moment's silence in memory of the dear departed, he says:

—He was more than a mate. Only he had his life, and I had mine. If you think that I had anything to do with what happened to him, you're mistaken. Me, brother, I run a business. Honestly. For money, I roll up my sleeves, without ever drawing a gun. I'm not a killer.

—Your file suggests that you dabble in fundamentalism, probes Serdj.

Omar bursts into an exaggerated laugh. He starts swaying again:

—That's not my style, brother. Can you imagine me in the robe of an Afghan shepherd, me—who loves smart dressing?!

—You were flirting with Mourad…

—Stop! Mourad was my mate, brother. A kid from my neck of the woods. We were dying from hunger and we tightened our belts and helped each other. We were both born in the same cesspit and our mothers worked hard for the same broker. At that time we didn't have big appetites. Bits and pieces. Just enough to get by, get a change of breeches and fill ourselves at the cheapest eatery in town.

He seems sad; he finds it painful to rummage through the past. It was not pleasant, he adds. We didn't dare have our photo taken.

—That's why you shot yourself with hashish.

—I don't touch that filth. The dream, I consume it lucidly, brother. Who told you that crap?

—Slimane...Slimane Abbou, anticipates Serdj.

Omar frowns:

—Never heard of him.

—He pushes drugs around the *Casbah* area.

He shakes his head:

—Don't know him.

I slip an identikit picture of Didi under his nose:

—He's not a comic strip hero, I caution.

He pulls a face, scratches his ear, takes his time:

—Is it the Rambo of the cabaret in rue des Lauriers-roses?

—Absolutely right.

—I run across him from time to time at the sea front. We don't greet each other.

—You haven't seen him lately?

—Not that I've noticed.

—And Brahim Boudar? Serdj hurries him.

But he won't be hurried, Malkom aka Iks. He replies slowly, quite detached:

—He's a nothing. We met in prison. Promiscuity, whatever. He's not my cup of tea...

—He's dead.

—None too soon.

—Nevertheless, with Boudar, Daho Lamine and Mourad Atti, it was going well for you.

He stops me. His ring-laden fingers hide his face: Let's

understand each other, brother. Let's not confuse *Ramadan* and *Sha-ban*.* Daho Lamine was rich, a regular goldmine for Mourad and me. The first time we set foot in a real restaurant, it was with him. He was running a smuggling ring and offered us simple jobs carrying suitcases. Just rags. One trip to Alicante, another to Marseilles or Damascus, and a solid envelope on our return. That's how I was able to pay for a small shop at the bottom of the rue de Oiseleours. Hell—I knew I was running risks. When the customs officers intercepted me, I didn't complain. One doesn't get something for nothing.

—Daho was in arms trafficking...

—That was his business. It's not my cup of tea. Me, I only did rags. No drugs, no cars. Just rags.

I nod my head in assent. Serdj comes up to take over from me.

—How was it, October 1988?

With his finger, Omar signals to him that he's seen it coming. He executes a dance step, spills out his milky smile and relates: Mourad found me in my shop. He was excited. He said to me: 'Can you keep this quiet?' I said 'I want to see first of all.' He said to me: 'We're going to raise bedlam in the town.' I said: 'It's already a mess.' He said: 'Exactly. There's going to be a roughhouse on a big scale. The street won't know itself afterward. Piece of cake. You invest in a box of matches and you come home with 25,000 francs.' At that time, 25,000 didn't build you a facade, but it got the construction work under way. I said 'Done!' Two days later the street was overflowing everywhere. We set fire to shops and buses. We were arrested and thrown into jail. For my part, I paid cash, without any remission of sentence.

—Who was behind all the chaos?

—You disappoint me, brother.

—And after?

—After what, brother?

—Daho Lamine became a fundamentalist.

—We didn't wear the same fez.

—But you knew what was going on in his head?

—It was crystal clear. Daho would do business with Mephistopheles. He was protecting his rear. They were counting heavily on the fundamentalists and he didn't fancy being hung on a gibbet with the renegades.

—And Brahim Boudar?

—A born killer, he said, sweeping the air with a gesture of disgust. Even as a kid, he martyred the cats and dogs. No dog would risk its hide in our neighborhood.... Of course he tried to recruit me. I dotted the 'i's' for him. No blood on my hands. Your brother, friend, is like the sparrow: he builds his nest, little by little. I know there is a tribunal, up there. I told Mourad the same thing. But Mourad adored make-believe. He was getting his revenge on the foundry; he didn't retain a single verse of religion. He believed in a single god, the only god who does not require prophets to do his publicity—money!

Serdj is not convinced. He ploughs on: As a rule the fundamentalists eliminate those who don't agree with them.

—I got out early. Right after the suspension of the electoral process, I felt it was going to turn out badly. There was too much manipulation in the air.

—Meaning what?

—Hard to explain. I didn't like it. I find it hard to imagine guys at the bar and the *minbar** at the same time. It wasn't *Sunni*. Notorious evildoers in the shirts of *Mullahs* didn't look at all good to me. It was as if a Trojan horse was invading the mosques...listen, brother, I'm no cop or reporter—I'm a shopkeeper.

—You have no idea about Mourad's death?

—A thousand and one ideas. Mourad was a skirt chaser. He mounted both virgins and wives. Inevitably, the jealous husbands would be wise to him...

—Did he ever mention a certain Abou Kalybse to you?

—He didn't have to. Abou Kalybse is the emir in fashion. His posters are hanging everywhere. They say that he attacks only the intelligentsia.

—Did Mourad know him?

—Listen, brother, we aren't going to spend the night here. I've got other things to do. Mourad didn't confide everything to me. He came mainly to elicit my admiration. It annoyed him to live pleasantly without me at his side. Me, I don't take risks. Little by little, but one holds on to one's life.

—Abou Kalybse…just content yourself with answering the question.

Omar shakes his shoulders, runs a big tongue over his lips and jingles his rings on the counter. He wises up.

—Mourad knew him, that's certain. He often said 'With Abou Kalybse every gram of intellectual's brain is worth its weight in gold.' But he didn't go any further with his confidences…is that enough, brother? In any case, I've emptied my sack.

I thank him, request that Serdj walk out in front of me. Before the inspector puts his hand on the door handle, I turn round to face the cousin from the Bronx:

—One *nota bene** and I sign out. What is it exactly, the Limbes?

His cheekbones tremble:

—The most beautiful woman in the world can only give what she has, brother. There are taboos. One must respect them. I have a young kid, and I'm attached to him.

—Are you afraid?

—That's it. I'm shitting in my pants, if you must know. The last idiot to frequent that joint has balls so enormous that a wicker basket wouldn't be big enough to hold them.

—It's bizarre nonetheless. The emir of the *Casbah* worked there as a dishwasher. Didi as a bouncer. Mourad, Brahim Boudar…what is it, that dunghill? A terrorist factory?

Omar swallows. He looks unhappy. He groans:

—I've got to close. I've been cooperative and sweet, brother. Now, please go.

Chapter fourteen

The weirdest dream kept me tense all night long. I was bouncing along on a powdery track. I was cold, and the moon was trickling like a Camembert cheese onto my windscreen. Ragged and sinister trees turned away as I passed. I had no idea where I was headed for. In my driving mirror, two dull eyes observed me.

At the bend of a bridge I fell upon an interminable line of fundamentalists, their chests bristling with bandoleers and beards down to their knees. Everything was pointing the way to a wood peopled by as many ventripotent ogres as tree trunks. Suddenly my headlights fastened on a kind of Goliath armed with an ax bigger than my terror. At the same moment the eyes in my driving mirror ejected themselves and came, with a dreadful humming, to consume mine. I screamed…and Mina almost hit the ceiling.

—I had a nightmare, I tried to calm her.

She went straight back to sleep. As for myself, with my stomach churning, I counted off the minutes one by one until the call of the *muezzin*.

Lino didn't come to fetch me. I waited for him for a full hour, transfixed behind the window, a nauseous foreboding in my throat. A neighbor agreed to drop me off at the station.

Bliss is waiting for me on the steps, looking very distressed. I realize that something bad has happened.

—Serdj has been reported missing, he reluctantly informs me.

My department resembles a mortuary. Baya is sniffling into a handkerchief, her eyelids puffed up. The orderly reminds one of a gravedigger. The men in uniform listen sadly to plainclothes men. There's silence as I enter. Lino is dehydrating behind his typewriter, his chin in his palms, staring vacantly.

—What happened to him?

Bliss is the first to react: The commander of the 13th Regiment just reported to us that Serdj's burned out car was found in the vicinity of Doar Nemmiche. The inspector must have been kidnapped at a false roadblock.

—What the hell was he doing in Doar Nemmiche? Everyone knows that it's a veritable snake pit, that it's crawling with fundamentalist vermin.

—He had a phone call from his brother. His father passed away the day before.

My hands gesture aimlessly. My knees threaten to give way. I collapse in a chair and sink into a state of incapacity. Through my numb fog I hear Bliss adding: The regiment is on the spot. It's conducting a sweep of the area.

One hour elapses, then a second, a third. The director is distraught. Ceaselessly he makes the journey from the third floor to the ground floor to inquire about the situation.

—Serdj won't give in without a struggle, says a policeman in the corridor, *sotto voce*.

—Sure he retaliated, intones the orderly. Serdj is a man. He won't let himself be kidnapped. Sure he defended himself. If he's dead, they must have shot him. Serdj is no lamb.

What a strange era we live in! When a colleague is shot dead, that's considered the best thing that could have happened to him—in view of the horribly dismembered cadavers littering the unfortunate land of Algeria. Toward midday the telephone shrills, paralyzing us all. Bliss hands me the phone.

—The regiment.

The receiver burns my fists.

—Superintendent Llob.

—Yes.

—Commander Hamid of the 13th Regiment. I am so sorry…(I fall back in my seat)…we found him in a small mosque.…

I feel like crushing the receiver, the office, the whole world.

—Are you there, Superintendent?

—Oh no! Oh God no!

—Truly sorry.

—Did he suffer?

—He is no longer suffering. It won't bring him back, but my men killed three of the nine kidnappers. We'll go on till we track down the rest of the band.

—Thank you, Commander.

As I put down the receiver, Baya buries her head in her hands and emits a piercing and unbearable howl.

ン

Serdj's body is brought back in the late afternoon. At the morgue, the director advises me strongly to let the surgeon do his work.

—I'd rather you remember him as he was—a good coworker, Llob. He's been so damaged. They're sewing his head back on his trunk now.

The following day all Serdj's colleagues assemble at Bab el Oued for the funeral service. The street is thronged with neighbors, young people from the neighborhood, old-timers and curious onlookers. Lieutenant Chater has deployed two security cordons and stationed marksmen on the surrounding rooftops. The terrorists have got us used to unimaginable humiliations. They will kill a mother solely to trap the son the day the body is buried, or assassinate a cop to machine-gun down his colleagues who have come to gather by his graveside. However, the director, local authorities, and officers of the 13th regiment all insist on offering their condolences to the family of the deceased. I arrive last, because of Lino, who has disappeared.

A child is playing with a bicycle wheel on the road, not at all impressed by the crowd. He must be five or six years old. He's Serdj's youngest son, an uncle informs me. He is unaware that all the people are there for him. They lead me into a small house. I finally understand why Serdj never invited me home. He must have wanted not to embarrass me. His hovel is so insalubrious that the occupants seem frailer than phantoms.

Our friend is committed to a dilapidated cemetery. Yesterday they buried the father, today the son. Thus goes the *sunna** of life.

Someone mutters to me:

—God is great.

—So is hell, I retort.

The *imam** raises his voice in the *fatiha** prayer. I raise my eyes skyward. When they begin to throw earth onto my colleague's body, a cloud stops under the sun, as if casting a piece of night on the career of a cop.

※

All that day, I searched for Lino. At Da Achour's, in the eateries, by the brothels. Then I remembered the back room of the shop of Sid-Ali, a retired instructor. The higher ranks meet at weekends at his place to down a few liters and exchange the latest gossip.

Sid-Ali thrusts his thumb over his shoulder. He's taken it very badly, he confides to me.

—He's not the only one.

Lino is sprawled over a table, his cheek under his arm. The number of overturned beer cans gives an idea of the extent of the damage. I cough into my fist. Lino reacts feebly. He forages in his disheveled hair, and smiles at me via a glass. It's not exactly a smile, just the grimace of a man who hasn't managed to recover his faculties. He shakes his watch, lifting it to his ear.

—Have you wound your watch? he mumbles.

—My watch is a quartz.

—Mine has stopped.

—Life goes on.

He's drunk as a lord, Lino. He's completely let himself go in his slovenly suit. His gestures are incoherent and his tongue wedges against his gums like a rusty latch.

—You call this a life, Super? A stay of execution at best. Why have you come to adulterate my wine?

—Because getting sozzled isn't going to get you anywhere.

He suddenly overturns the table, staggers. I try to hold him up. He pushes my hand away with a horrified gesture:

—I am still capable of standing upright, ho! I stand so straight on my legs that at my funeral they will have to bury me standing.

—Stop acting the fool. We're going home.

—I don't have a home any more.

—This is a bad scene, Lino.

—Coward! He pushes me aside, staggers out to the street, and funneling his hands, he begins to shout:

—I'm a cop, hey! I'm not afraid. I'm a cop, come and get me.

I try to calm him down. He pushes me away:

—Take your hands off me, you! Don't touch me! Understand? Don't you see that you're not wanted around here? This evening you're in my way. Leave me alone, okay? And stop looking at me as if I am to be pitied. It's you who are to be pitied. You think you're on the right side. It's all so much a matter of chance…wherever you happen to be. In a good spot or a lousy spot. I'm no hero. I'm not even sure if I'm brave. I refuse to believe in the culture of cemeteries. I want to save my skin.

—You'll tell me that later.

He recoils, swaying:

—Just look at you…white as a sheet! He wipes his nose on an arm. You don't have a single drop of blood left. Is it the neighborhood that bothers you? I thought you had them in bronze. It's wild how you disappoint me.

A fine rain spits down on the city, but it's the liquids squirting out of the lieutenant's mouth that spray me. A young bearded fellow in a loose shirt comes out of a beauty shop. Lino waits for him to draw level before striking him with his fist.

—Filthy terrorist! Charnel house fly! Fucking *mullah*!*

I grip the lieutenant by the arms. He resists, charges at the stupefied little Brother. There follows an exchange of crude expletives, kicks in the air and gobs of spit. The little Brother rolls up his fez and the sleeves of his shirt. I grab him with one hand and back him up against the wall:

—Get lost.

—Is he cuckoo or what?

—Get lost quick before I belt you with the pubic hairs you have on your chin. I catapult the lieutenant into my jalopy and drive off. During the trip Lino is huddled in a corner of the back seat, his chin between his thighs and his hands on his head, and he bawls like a dozen babies.

Chapter fifteen

I had never suspected Lino capable of such wretchedness and sorrow. For three days and three nights he didn't have a single nice word to say about anything.

Absent from the canteen, poring over briefings, he spent more time drowning his sorrows in the company of his typewriter than he did taking an interest in the rest of the world. On several occasions I found him addressing himself in the toilets, his nose pressed against the mirror. He started to find fault with the personnel, unfailingly discovering a pretext to fulminate. He was unrecognizable.

I offered him leave, but he yelped back, outraged:

—I don't need any relaxation! We have the whole of eternity for that.

—I know what you're going through, I offered. I feel exactly the same. Serdj was our family. Fate decreed that he should be the first to go.

—You call that fate?

—Call it what you like. The fact remains: Serdj is dead. He didn't deserve to finish up this way. He was a fine person. At times I find it so unjust that I am on the verge of losing my faith. I also get some stupid ideas. I feel like drawing my gun and mowing down the first guy with a beard that crosses my path. If I don't do it, it's because that is not the done thing. I am not an assassin. I don't want to sink to their level. We have to remain ourselves, simple folk, but with hearts.

For a full minute, Lino remains speechless. One of his hands soundlessly smacks the other hand. Then his finger settles on my chest, tries to pierce it.

—I won't be fooled any longer. I know what's good and what isn't! The prevailing fucking wisdom of the country won't change anything! From now on I'm only doing what I want.

He storms out, slamming the door. I can't do very much for him. Every time I approach, he threatens to smack me in the face. One morning, in the middle of a work session, he decided to visit Serdj's grave. He didn't reach the cemetery. On the way he jumped a red light and rammed into a policeman.

The fourth day I took him out. We went to grill sausages at Da Achour's. Lino had become a loner: he remained apart. He stayed on the beach from morning to nightfall, throwing pebbles at the waves. Afterward, things improved. The sea calmed him down a bit.

⁂

Slimane Abbou has regained some color. A dressing on his chest, his hand attached to a sort of flushing system, he grimaces and then sinks back against the pillow. The doctor advises us not to press him too hard since complications could develop, and I promise him solemnly that I'll be cool, and I wait till he leaves the room before pulling up a chair in a convivial way up to the side of the bed on which our dealer is convalescing.

—Well, how's the lung?

—They repaired it, but I get short of breath now and again.

Lino prefers to observe the white uniforms in the courtyard through the window. He grunts without turning round:

—You should have brought him candies, Super.

Slimane starts fidgeting:

—What's he got against me, your guy?

—Forget about him. How about telling us your story from the beginning?

—I haven't enough saliva. And then, with my gasping for air...

—We went and had a look round your cabin.

—Hey, easy. That wasn't my cabin. It belonged to Moh Lakja.

—And you shot the guy with the club foot?

—It was an accident. I wanted to help him up and the gun went off.

—You're damned right. It *was* an accident. We were there and you can count on our testimony.

He sniggers. There's enough cynicism to set your gums on edge:

—I knew you were a good guy. Otherwise I wouldn't have missed you.

—What were you manufacturing, at Moh Lajka's?

—I was giving him his dose of medicine.

—He's white as his coke, Lino comments ironically with his nose against the pane.

Slimane is annoyed. He raises himself on an elbow and brays:

—Yeah, I am white and I piss you off. Personally, I didn't have the luck to become a police officer or an executive.

—Careful, I calm him down, or you'll puncture your inner tube.

But apparently my remarks have stimulated him. He sits up a bit more and vituperates:

—Turn around, dimwit. Look me in the eye, if you're a man at all. You despise me because I have no learning, is that it? Tell me: how does one eat when one has neither a diploma or a job? Do you know what it means to see your mother weep when we sit down at the table because she has nothing to put in the little ones' bowls? Do you know what it is to have to take refuge in the lumber-room because your father has come home drunk again? Do you know what it's like to get zeroes on your exam papers because at home there's such chaos that it would be stupid to review your lessons?

—Listen, we're not in court, I rein him in.

Slimane shuts up, breathless. Suddenly he bursts out laughing; a manic laugh that makes your blood run cold:

—Nevertheless, he sniggers, it worked every time with the judge.

I have a hard time controlling my anger. I struggle to keep my *sangfroid*. Slimane is as stubborn as a mule. It is useless to remind him of it.

—You're in the shit up to your neck, I inform him. Your weapon has been identified. It belonged to a magistrate assassinated at Tamalous. We also know that you extorted protection money from a host of shopkeepers and kidnapped two sisters. You sell drugs for the benefit of armed groups. We have proof. We know that Didi is your buddy and that Abou Kalybse is your guru.

He listens, his eyebrows knitted affectedly, fluttering his eyelids as when one makes eyes comically, as if to make it clear to me that my remarks amuse him and that he couldn't care a fig about my charge list.

—How much will I get, cop?

—You are of no interest to us.

—How nice! A little earlier you put such fear into me, you know.

—The albino, is he one of your clients?

—Is that a code name?

—The fellow who drove the Mercedes. We saw him drop you off at Didi's little girlfriend's place.

—Are you referring to the excitable guy without pigmentation? They call them albinos? I didn't know. In my opinion he's one of the Securité people. He knew me better than my mother. He forced me to take him to Yasmina. Yasmina didn't know much. So then he got angry, the albino, and he hit her very hard. He wanted to go right up to Abou Kalybse.

—And he spared you?

—It's not the same thing. We did a deal. The albino made me a great offer if I managed to show him a way. I went round to Lajka to negotiate. Lajka wasn't any better informed. Nothing is known about Abou Kalybse except the rustling of the fax…I was going to be set for good, I swear it. With my commission I envisaged finding myself a small business, having kids and turning over a new leaf. Two hundred thousand he promised me, the albino. And you cut the grass from under my feet.

—'scuse us, mocks Lino, we weren't well informed.

Slimane contemplates his nails as he reflects: Is it true that you execute terrorists?

—What do you think?

—I wish to repent. Is it feasible?

—What do you think? snaps Lino.

—On my mother's life, I've never met Abou Kalybse. He contacts me by fax. Afterward I go to pick up my pay from Didi.

—Where is Didi?

—No idea.

—In hiding?

—Didi, in hiding? He's incapable of surviving far from a good bed and a bath.

—Is he your cashier? Or what, exactly?

—A post box.

—And who is the mailman?

At this, Slimane is fully awake. His beyond-the-grave pupils emit sparks: Your question has a price, cop.

—Can we do a deal?

He relaxes, passes his hand under the nape of his neck, crosses his legs under the sheets and gazes dreamily at the ceiling. I feel like tearing out his guts. He yaps:

—I demand to be released.

—Is that all?

—Hee, hee! He starts to snigger again. A hyena would find it hard to imitate him.

—Release me or nothing!

Suddenly Lino tears himself away from the window, leaps at Slimane and begins to pummel his wound ferociously. The shouts and insults reverberate throughout the block. The doctor and the nurses invade the room in a whirlwind of feet and hands to put a stop to the lieutenant's devastating fury.

Terrified, Slimane begs:

—Get that lunatic out of here and I'll tell you everything!

Chapter sixteen

In Algiers there are days when the sky and the sea conspire to induce a feeling of unbelievable plenitude. It's blue as far as the sea, and even in the very depths of winter, the rebellious and facetious sun manages to restore the summer. Of all the suns on this earth ours is the only one that successfully performs this sleight of hand.

Everything seems serene once again. One hears the birds warbling and the foliage rustling. The air is a marriage of warm currents and delicate scents. One feels like dozing off and never waking. No doubt about it: Paradise comes from God. Hell it is man-made.

It's very beautiful, *Algiers la Blanche*, when the atmosphere is so limpid that one can distinguish an oak from a carob tree for miles around. If it weren't for those inconvenient killings and that colony of deluded luminaries which feed on the streets and the minds, one would not exchange Algiers for a thousand magnificent spectacles. From the balcony where I am reclining, I contemplate the *Casbah* tucked into its reef to escape the raids of the low tides. Bab el Oued reminds one of a barracks on a day off, and the port lower down seems just like a tavern bar where bribes change hands. Even when something that glitters is not gold, it is nonetheless fascinating for us…but there is Omar Malkom, who is bleeding from the nose, and his bellowings dispel my reveries. He is on all fours, one eye blackened and teeth loosening, while, in a frenzy of fury, Lino rearranges his face.

—Well then, like that brother, 'little by little, you build your nest.' Isn't that what he said, right Super?

—May I go to hell if I lie, I confirm.

Lino lifts his shoe and smashes it on the punk's fingers.

—Your celebrity outfit, I'm going to turn it into a dishrag.

—You're on the wrong track. Slimane is jealous of my success. He told you a load of bull! I'm a businessman. I earn my money honestly.

—How did he put it, Super?

—'Little by little, and one holds on to one's life.'

—Apparently, he isn't holding on to it any longer, to his whore's life.

—He thinks maybe that you're fooling him and that, for lack of evidence, you'll let him go in the end.

—Well, he's wrong.

Lino steps back, winds himself up and fires with all his might. Omar crumples up in pain, his hands on his stricken kidney.

—You are torturing me. You have no right. It's against the law.

—No sweat. With the *fatwa* that your gurus have issued against foreigners, there's no chance of Amnesty International coming to your rescue.

I go back inside the room, seize the punk by his pitiful tuft of hair and stuff my breath up his nostrils:

—I've got the time. You're going to spill everything, even if to get there I have to make omelets out of your balls. Don't try blurring the tracks. I have you by the tail and I won't let you go. The sooner you deliver, the sooner you'll be relieved.

—I'm in business.

—I want to kiss Abou Kalybse. It's personal, you get it?

—I'm in business.

—Out of the way, Super.

A spray of blood splatters my knee when the lieutenant's fist smashes into the punk's discomposed face.

—I am a businessman, he insists. I don't ask for the moon. I'm satisfied with what I have. I'm not greedy. You're making a mistake, boys. I'm in business.

We lift him up and attach him to a chair.

—No point in trying to blur the tracks, I'm telling you. You are the treasurer and sworn recruiter of Abou Kalybse.

—It's not true.

—It is true.

—It's not true, it's not true, it's not true...

He sticks to his *leitmotif* for hours on end. Lino's fists are bruised at the joints. His blotch-speckled shirt steams in the furnace. Exhausted, I sit in an armchair to recuperate.

—How about trying Article 220 of the Code of Accelerated Procedure, a panting Lino suggests to me.

Although groggy, Omar knits his brow:

—Eh, brother, what is he on about? I'm not a guinea pig.

Lino tears out the TV plug and begins to strip the wires.

—Have you ever tried to shave your anus with a pair of pliers? No? Then how can I explain to you what Article 220 of the Code is?

Omar Malkom is at the end of his tether. He breathes laboriously. With an exhausted hand he begs the lieutenant to pack up his gear.

—That's it, brother, I give in. God is my witness; I've held out to the very limit of my powers.

—The Devil must be proud of you.

He sags against the back of the chair, totally spent, on the verge of passing out.

—Slimane maintains that it was you who liquidated Sabrine Malek.

—That's a lie. It's true that I kept her locked up, but I didn't kill her.

—Why did they kidnap her?

—It's Mourad Atti's fault. He shouldn't have fallen for that bitch. She wasn't a part of the harem. At the club the instructions are clear: no intruders…Mourad let himself be seduced by the false ingenuousness of the prostitute. Then it turned out that the tramp was no ordinary prostitute. It was a trick. Someone had planted her in the team, to get to the guru. Abou Kalybse got wind of it. He had her abducted. She stayed in a shed for a week. Then someone came to collect her. I haven't seen her since.

—Mourad was executed for that little slip.

—He was beginning to stumble too often. It's unhealthy for a family of tightrope walkers like the club. From the start I had the feeling that we were balancing along a razor's edge. But with this kind of internal behavior, there's no turning back.

—Did you know who Sabrine was?

—The daughter of an old power broker. She told me. I couldn't do anything for her. In the trenches, one looks after one's helmet and flask. The rest one entrusts to the good graces of the Lord.

—Who were the two guys who made out they were agents of the Obs?

—No idea. Abou Kalybse has warning bells on every corner.

—What's the general idea behind your club?

—Meaning?

—Who are you? Fundamentalists? A secret society? What is your leaning? Is it political, religious, mystical…?

He wipes his bloodied lips on his arm, probes his teeth. His chest flutters painfully.

—I have no idea. I needed money. The first one who proposed it to me recruited me. Our club deals with the intellectuals. Others, with industrialists. Others still, with the magistrature. It's war, and also a god-sent opportunity to settle your scores and clean up. Personally, I have nothing against the academics. I don't even know what they represent; but I keep the cashbox, brother. They send me a fax: such and such a sum for so and so. I have him sign a receipt which I return by fax, and I go home. It's not that I don't care. I have nothing in particular to reproach myself with. I'm simply a teller, a simple automatic dispenser…personally, I have a hatred of firearms…

—Where does our man hide out?

He carefully presses his fist against his torn lip and says in a gurgle: Pavillon 17, Deheb neighborhood, on the mountain road.

Then, exorcised, he starts to weep nervously.

I seize the phone and call the office. It's Bliss who lifts the receiver.

—What are you doing in my quarters?

—I was passing and heard the phone ringing. Since no one was answering, well....

—I have reminded you a hundred times not to go near my desk when I'm not in the office. Okay, we need a hiding place at 162, rue des Freres-Adou. We're talking about a big fish. You'll put him in cold storage and don't speak of it to anyone.

—Not even to the director? he inquires, snakelike.

—A hiding place, and make it snappy.

❧

The Deheb neighborhood hasn't got a clear conscience. It lies hidden in a fold of the mountain, behind the hills, and makes out it isn't there. It's a tranquil bay consisting of some thirty villas bisected by a wide, straight road with young palm trees and cast-iron lampposts on each side. It is one of those parcels of land which are passed surreptitiously among the corrupt police in the administration, directly and without fanfare so as not to arouse any unwelcome curiosity—fabulous oases sold for a symbolic dinar and which one keeps under wraps like a national security secret. To unearth it, one has to be an old hand at this type of hide and seek. From the main road one cannot even see the slip road which the bushes devour, and which nonetheless wends its unobtrusive way behind them before plucking up courage a few hundred meters further on, being covered with a protective coating of asphalt, and charging onto the smooth sand of the beach, and thence onto this microcosm of the fortunate few.

When I think of the dormitory cities which pervert our landscapes, and the insipid 'tenement blocks', no sooner launched than already fallen into decay, and become breeding grounds for hostilities; when I think of the shantytowns that continue to extend into the very mentalities of the people, the basement windows gaping onto sulfuric emanations, I don't harbor too many illusions about the days that lie ahead.

※

Lino has given up his excesses of adolescent adulation. The riches of others—he knows what that is. Lino is a hardened individual now. Soured, but hardened. He took some time to understand, but he got there. Pessimistically, he now disdains the arrogance of palaces and confines himself to just taking an interest in the numbers on their doors. Number Seventeen sits nonchalantly at the end of the road, its chin in a garden and its rear end on the sand. It's a real architectural jewel, with blue stone on the facade, arcades over the veranda and a front door comely as a trinket. Sid Lankabout keeps us hanging about for five minutes before opening the door.

—Llob? he frowns.

—Surprised?

—Absolutely. What wind has blown you this way?

—The wind that turns, Monsieur Lankabout.

He smoothes down the front of his dressing gown, eyes Lino disdainfully.

—I cannot receive you. I am writing now.

—You will have all the time to polish your moral discourse in prison.

His right eyebrow twitches. Imperceptibly. The rest remains unmoved.

—I see, he says.

It's clear that he believes that by maintaining his *sangfroid*, I will be convinced that he has character. His long concubinage with the bigwigs of the regime confers on him a superficial, theatrical majesty. He guesses the object of my visit, however the contempt he has for me forbids him to betray the slightest emotion.

I push past him and enter the dwelling. The salon is chockfull of a panoply of electronic gadgets, computer programs, faxes and radios which turn the place into a command headquarters.

—Is this your apocalyptic laboratory, Monsieur Abou Kalybse?

—I have considerably underestimated you, Llob.

—The cop or the novelist?

—Both. Each time I was going to put your name on my black list, my categorical refusal to acknowledge any talent in you dissuaded me. Simultaneously, I have amused myself by putting to the test your reputation as a shrewd detective.

I signal to Lino to go and inspect the upstairs floor. Sid Lankabout settles himself behind his desk; he has stiffened perceptibly, caressing the leaves of his inspirations.

—It was a fine novel, he sighs.

—That's what one inevitably tells oneself before the reading committee's report.

On the walls hang the portraits of recently assassinated intellectuals: Abou Kalybse's hunting scene. Here are the trophies of his sinister glory: three writers, four academics, a theocrat, five journalists, a comedy actor and a university lecturer. I linger on the burlesque grimace of my late departed friend Ait Meziane. My heart contracts like a fist.

—What a waste!

Sid Lankabout collects his sheaf of pages, taps it to level it out. Behind him the window looks out onto a rock licked at by languorous waves.

He recites: 'God only ameliorates the condition of a people when he has corrected its mentality.'

—Perhaps it is yours that is defective.

—I don't think so. When I see all those bastardized people who impregnate our cities and towns, all those young people who become Americanized, all those intellectuals who strive to inculcate us with an alien culture by making us believe implacably that one Verlaine is worth ten Chawki, that one Pulitzer carries the weight of a hundred Akkads, that Gide represents the truth and Tewfik el Hakim only nonsense, that transcendence is Western and regression is Arabist, I do exactly what Goebbels would have done when facing Thomas Mann: I draw my gun.

He places his papers in a folder, deposits them in a drawer and finally looks up:

—Did one have to exorcise the demon or tame him? Imperatively a choice had to be made. One cannot tame the demon.

I point at the portraits: They were neither demons nor demented, Sid. They were ordinary people, innocent, ordinary people. They had children, hopes, legitimate ambitions and wished nobody any harm.

—Rubbish! When I took up arms against the French colonialists, it was not for a chimera. I dreamed of an Algerian Algeria, with its Koranic *mederassas*,* mosques, turbaned sages. I dreamed of a land proud of it identity, its history, its soil, recognizable among a thousand others: proud of its accents, its tongue, and its traditions.... And what do I see? An Algiers as depraved as an overseas metropolis, a people devoid of personality, heretical universities, a destiny that has slid into mortal triviality.

He points contemptuously to his victims:

—They were not decent, Llob. They were deceitful, perfidious, destructive. They were like moths. They were our enemies. Traitors. They were in the pay of the renegades, of the henchmen of Satan.

—Ait Meziane was barely able make ends meet. He died in debt up to the gravestone.

—He was a mediocre acrobat. He embodied the type of Algerian, debunker of myths, simplifier and negativist, which we reject. It could not last. The ridicule was overflowing the rubbish dumps. It became imperative to burn the forest so that in its place another would arise, cleared of vermin, disinfected, robust...

There's no doubt about it, the man talking to me is mad. I look at his cheeks, his gleaming eyes with their dilated pupils, the sweat streaming from his temples, his fingers and his vocal chords trembling.

—*You* have always detested solid values, Sid, because *you* are an absurdity. I've got your number—you're spiteful, austere, allergic to good humor. You're a killjoy. You can't stand other peoples' success. Their very sense of vocation tortures your susceptibilities. It is because you are a born unfortunate for whom nothing has any visible meaning. You speak to me of your dreams, and it is the nightmare that surfaces. A horrifying spider ensconced at the bottom of its web, that's what you are. You are envious of every writer, of every performer who steals the limelight from you. All your life you have sought to overhang the world, to radiate over it, not thanks to your genius—of which you are totally devoid—but because of the pyre of your hostilities. You've been the factotum of tyrants, enthroned not to instruct and guide, but to obscure the true elite like some tree which pollutes the forest. By dint of indulging in falsehood, one can no longer do without it. Your 'friends' of the old regime used you—your egocentrism, your megalomania. They set you against your natural allies, and against yourself. They got you used to the giddy heights, then they forgot you on a cloud. But you are neither God, nor an angel, Monsieur Sid Lankabout. You are just an illusion. You deserve the pity of the living as well as the dead….

He extends his hands to me, delivers them to me. I say to him:

—You don't need handcuffs. You don't even need a strait-jacket.

He looks at his hands, reverses them and puts his weight against them in order to stand up. Delicately. His fingers meet, intertwine. Sid must be thinking that he's at the front of a solemn auditorium, preparing to deliver a speech. The light from the window envelops him like a tunic of Nessos; he's the personification of inescapable misfortune. He is now no more than a phantom, a shadow that detaches itself from the day.

—Madness is what escapes the majority of mortals, he says, in a disembodied tone of voice. A wise man is mad when he manifests his erudition among the ignorant. Galileo was mad in the eyes of the Church. Ibn Sina was mad to profane the body of a human being. But the years bring unbearable revelations to the generations to come. Ingeniousness and ingenuousness, fallibility and viability, error and reason—these are made and unmade at the whim of sudden changes of mood. How many traitors of yesteryear are glorified today? How many absurd ideas have turned out to be astonishing prophecies? In reality, Llob, there is no absolute truth, nor fundamentally false untruth; there are only things that one believes in, and others in which one does not believe…

It is then that the window explodes. Sid Lankabout is hurled onto the desk, his skull torn off by a high caliber bullet. I glimpse a silhouette spring from behind the rock outside, and run toward the copse. Then I hear a car drive away with a discordant screech.

Chapter seventeen

The director insists on celebrating the demise of Abou Kalybse. He organizes a modest reception at headquarters, where he hosts the secretary of the administrative area, the superintendents, a handful of officers from the special units and a cluster of journalists. The Chief-of-Police couldn't make it, but nonetheless he delegated a tediously voluble representative, far more curious to see what the demolisher of the Beast looked like than to eulogize. The director glorifies my 'perseverance' and my 'sense of abnegation.' He calls me by my first name, and this makes me blush like a virgin presented with a hot dog.

Everyone is unanimous in acknowledging that Abou Kalybse was one hell of a catch. To hear them, one might think that terrorism had been eradicated. They shake my hand, tap me on the shoulder, rain triumphant jabs on my paunch—and not one of them thinks of congratulating Lino. Lino is almost ashamed of being among us, he, the thingified subaltern, the unsung and undeserving bearer. Yet this doesn't seem to affect him unduly. Lino knows that in a society where one rarely says *Thanks!* and never *Excuse me* ingratitude is second nature. Later, he confides to me that, in his situation of enforced celibacy, he would willingly exchange all the honors of the world for a modest two-rooms-plus-kitchen apartment in which to start a family. May Saint Glinglin hear him. From his mouth to God's ear! At home, the kids are fretting in front of the TV. On our 'Grosses Tête' political satire program they are arguing over an anecdote so boring that my daughter threatens to go into a fit of depression. I hang my jacket on a nail and install myself in the kitchen. Mina presents me with onion soup furrowed with vermicelli. She doesn't look well, my beast of burden. So much awkwardness at the end of the gesture, so many evasive looks. I seize her by the wrist. She resists, refuses to sit on my knees.

—You don't look yourself, my dear.

She raises a worried hand to her forehead.

—Your little exploit has been on the air. It's all over the radio.

—Did they mention my name?

—No, but it amounts to the same thing.

She is very upset. That's how she is all the time. Her eldest son has left, her oldest daughter is moping for lack of a suitor, and her husband is the lead poster at the terrorist Olympics. When I go out she waits by the window, when I'm five minutes late, she goes out of her mind. She's going to pieces, Mina. Her contours, which once excelled in synchronizing my pulse to her swinging hips, have become shapeless. Her heart beats only with fear and fury.

—Don't take it to heart, dear. Everything will be okay.

❧

Toward three in the morning the phone exacerbates my insomnia. I lift the receiver.

—Hello, *habibo*,* barks a disguised voice. You did a good job. I thank you. You have extracted a thorn from my foot…. Are you all right, not too tired? I'll bet you were having nightmares.

—You did well to call. I was about to die from fear.

—Ah! yes…

He hangs up. Mina moves beneath the covers.

—Who was that?

—A claustrophobic night watchman.

She raises herself on an elbow. Her eyes glisten in the dark:

—Someone hasn't stopped ringing since the morning.

—Go back to sleep.

She obeys.

I grope on the bedside table, find a cigarette, light it. In the next room my youngest son is delirious for ten seconds then is silent. The night is blue-tinted on the windowpanes. A piece of the moon hankers after its fullness in the sky. Once again, the phone.

—It's me again, *habibo.*

—You took the wrong tablet, is that it?

—It's my temperament. It amuses me to chat with my prey before I kill it. It brings us a little closer, make us familiar with each other. I hate to dispatch a guy without knowing him. That leaves me with a feeling of incompleteness. Hey! What can you do? Not all people are the same.

—Who is this speaking?

—Surely not interference on the line, *habibo.*

—Is this a joke?

—My *compadres* actually find my humor underdeveloped. The other day, the fellow whose throat I was about to slit couldn't find anything better to elicit my compassion than to point out to me that he had chronic pharingitis (laughs). Are you still there, *habibo*? So, why aren't you coughing any more? (laughs). Ciao!

My cigarette burns out in my fingers. I don't feel anything. I sit up on my butt and stare at the phone until dawn. Habibo didn't call back.

—You're so pale, Mina declares when she sees me first thing in the morning.

—Look, don't start, please.

I eat a hasty breakfast. My slice of bread sticks in my throat. I don't know why, suddenly the smell of butter makes me feel like vomiting. At the garage the guard makes the same remark to me:

—You're pale, Monsieur Superintendent.

—I put too much milk in my coffee.

I inspect the parking lot, look under the cars, approach my

Zastava, and check it without touching the handles, on the lookout for a stray wire, then I peek under the hood. No sign of a bomb.

—Are you sure you're OK, the watchman inquires.

—Are you a doctor?

—No…

—Then what are you so curious about?

The watchman buries his nose in the fold of his neck and disappears. I settle into the driving seat, take my courage in both hands, and turn the ignition key. The motor roars at a quarter turn. Curiously. As a rule, it is recalcitrant. It is only when I grip the gear lever that I discover, scrawled on the driving mirror: *T'est mort habibo!* ("You're dead, friend!").

If Bliss were to tell my worst enemies that Llob is a tire, that a nothing deflates him, no one would take him seriously. Nevertheless, for the space of a pinch, I have the impression that the sky is falling on my head.

❧

Habibo rejoins me at the office:

—Did you find my message?

—T'est is written with "es."

—Well, seeing that it's not my language…

—What do you want?

—To amuse myself with you. I was in the garage. I had a good laugh. Your poor wagon, the valves were damaged. You must be asking yourself where I was hiding, hey, *habibo*? You looked everywhere. That shows how smart I am. I could easily have shot you, but I am going to make you suffer. You are going to plead with me to finish you off. I adore being pleaded with. I love it. Often, I let the prey see a small light. It clings to it with all its might. It drags itself towards the door. In its head it thinks I have left. Then it drags itself bleeding, to the door, sees the stairs, the neighbor's door. Only three more meters, only two, only one. It lifts its hand just like one lifts up an anvil, scratches at the neighbor's door, again and yet again…. Finally the door opens, and the neighbor…is me.

He unleashes his deadly laugh. Half an hour later Mina calls me:

—Someone's put a parcel in front of our door.

—For goodness sake don't touch it, I shout. And keep your cool. Relax. Take the kids and get out. No hysteria, dear. Alert the neighbors. Everyone has to evacuate the building. I'm on my way.

> ❦

The parcel is on my doorstep. Two police sappers are examining it in an unbearable silence. The police have cordoned off the street. Mina and the children shiver in a paddy wagon, deathly pale and dumbstruck. I scrutinize the area. I feel Habibo very close, within reach of my gob of spit. And all the faces look suspicious to me. The two sappers finish dissecting the parcel. They emerge from the building, causing those gathered around it to fall back.

—False alarm, the senior sapper informs me.

In the parcel I find soap for my mortuary toilet, a shroud and a rosary. An old local custom. I take Lino aside confidentially and tell him:

—Quickly, get hold of my cousin Kader at Bejaia. Tell him that I'm sending Mina and the kids to him. No question of leaving them in Algiers.

Three days later, driving on the Zeralda road I am overtaken by a supercharged car. I was talking with Lino over the intercom and didn't notice the big sedan overtaking me. It suddenly swerved into my car door, jolting me from head to toe. The next thing I knew was the road rearing up, and the ditch sucking me up, then the void.

> ❦

—More fear than real damage, the doctor reassures me, echoing the clichés. You have a skull as solid as a convict's ball and chain.

I'm not certain whether this is meant as a compliment or a diagnosis, but I am extremely relieved. I get dressed in front of the mirror. The dressing enveloping my head makes me resemble a fakir whose tresses have got caught in a windmill.

Habibo calls me again at four in the morning.

—You almost ruined my evening.

—I shall pay more attention the next time, all right Didi?

He lets out a loud guffaw at the other end of the line: Didi is dead, *habibo*. He has been put in a hole and covered with reinforced concrete. The band of Sid Lankabout—*Kaput*! Only you and I are left. We are going to have the time of our lives. By the way, where did you send them to, your filthy urchins? I will find them. I will make pâté from their brains.

—Slow down a bit! You said that I was dead and I'm still alive.

—Not at all, you're dead. Really dead. It's you who reckons that you're still in this world. Your death certificate was signed at the same time as the contract. I have the reputation of burying my prey before it comes into the world.

—Prove it. I hang up.

He calls me back straight away:

—Filthy whoreson. I hate it when people hang up on me. Never do that to me again.

I tear out the telephone cable.

※

It's Monday. A sullen sky dispenses its moroseness over the town. The sun of my country is depressed. The atrocities that the night bequeaths it have triumphed over its magic. Every morning the radio informs us that a child has been killed, that a family has been decimated, that a train has been burned, that a part of the country has suffered a catastrophe. I pinch myself till I draw blood to ascertain that I am not dreaming. But it is not a bad dream. On the good and ancient land of Numidia, my brethren are well and truly killing one another, with a rare ferocity.

Of all peoples we are surely the 'most' extreme. We're either convinced that we're the best, or the worst. The happy medium—we don't know what that is. We have the bravest soldiers in the world, the most courageous women, and yet we count among our offspring the most fearful monsters on the planet. With us moderation is nonsense, a 'sub-appetite'. Perhaps this is why we remain as indomitable as we are unreasonable. Nonetheless, we persist in believing that a turnabout, a transformation, is possible, that from one moment to the next the hell of men will give way before the paradise of Allah, or that, from one border to the other, Algeria will become Algeria again, that is to say a territory where it may not be Sunday every day for sure, but where it feels good to live—a little anyhow, but to the full for sure.

A parsimonious rain lubricates the road. Dine chooses this moment to remember me.

—Llob, my beloved barrel, he exclaims at the end of the line, I hope I didn't wake you up.

—I'm in my office.

—Exactly, one can snooze better there. I called at your place. They told me that you had flown the coop.

—The area has become a shooting range.

—Ah! Ah! They've caught up with you, the snipers.

—What is it you want, retiree? A handshake or a kick?

Superintendent Dine coughs gently to clear his throat. He asks:

—Does my dossier still interest you?

—It might do. What's made you change your mind?

—Tahar Djaout.* He said: 'If you speak, you die. If you are silent, you die. So, speak and die.'

—I'll be with you in forty minutes.

I arrive there a quarter of an hour late. Police cars surround Dine's building. The sight of an ambulance freezes my blood. Shit, shit, shit!

Police signal to me to move back. The brigadier recognizes me and makes a police van reverse to let me through.

—Two terrorists tried to liquidate a colleague, the brigadier explains to me.

I leap from my seat. To my immense relief, Dine is standing in the stairwell, a gun in his hand. On the steps two contorted corpses spill out their venom, one with a dribbling poppy over his heart, the other with a strange freckle between his eyebrows.

—Llob, dear, either it's a coincidence, or you have been tapping my phone.

Chapter eighteen

The night returns at a gallop, its black cape flowing in the wind, the city lights reflected like sparks under its hoofs. Dine and I have opted for the home of Da Achour. His retreat permits us to concentrate and to delouse the dossiers at our leisure. We collate and check, reassess our information, run through video cassettes. The images parading before my eyes, the features emerging here and there, the congratulatory handshakes in the shadows stun me. It turns out that a large number of fundamentalists frequent the salons of the wealthy *nabobs*, are intimately familiar with the workings of the higher echelons. This one had been the bodyguard of such and such a director-general, and here he is now the emir of a cannibalistic horde. That one had been the chauffeur of a certain neo-bey, and here he is now circulating subversive tracts all over the country. As the revelations unfold, I am paralyzed by the feeling that seizes you by the throat when you perceive that the light at the end of the tunnel is only the reflection of Hell.

—From the outset, Dine relates, I knew that the death of Abbas Laouer was suspect. The banker was a hypochondriac. His medical register was kept better than a school detention register. As accurate as a Swiss clock. A medical examination every six months. Not an ounce of fat in excess, not a calorie too little. He was all set to beat the record for longevity. Yet at the cabaret they wouldn't let me within sight of the body. Haj Garne took the liberty of tearing up my search warrant. I thought that he had cooked his goose, but it was mine that went off the boil.

—It was the first time that I was conducting an investigation at that level, he continues. For a cop who had spent thirty years kicking the butts of petty criminals, it was hard to admit that there are people who exist above the law. I reopened the file on the Laouer affair, a case that was shelved almost before it began. The medical coroner's report confirmed a heart attack. I went to shake him up and it was he who threw me. My partner retired from the competition. It was all too evident, I simply lacked authority.

—So I went it alone. Judge Berrad encouraged me. But after three months I hadn't progressed one millimeter. That was when the first fuse blew in my head; I wanted to have the Limbes put under seal. The result: Haj turns up in person in my office, has me look at a video cassette. I recognized, shocked, my niece, in the center of a disgusting scene of debauchery. He left me the film as a sample and said to me: 'And what's more, I didn't look too carefully. There has to be a small documentary on your extra-marital adventures somewhere.'

—The huge sexual adventure, Llob. But I hung on. I tailed Soria Atti, alias Anissa. I took photos. The day I was convinced that I had her cornered, she laughed in my face. While I was unloading my compromising action shots on her bed, she switched on the video. And I saw Master Berrad, the doyen of the magistrature, in the process of being buggered in all his orifices by a minor. 'If I were you, I would give up the hunt for the unicorn,' Anissa told me. 'It would be nasty to be impaled on its horn.'

—This time I was alone, really alone. No more ally, no more support. I was furious. Haj Garne kept four luxury brothels supplied with prostitutes, had subscribers among the authorities, and ran a veritable porno videoteque to make them sing. Deputies, diplomats, councilors, jurists, journalists…. Just to rub it in, Garne assured me that he had slides on Adam and Eve. His industry was more than just a conservatory for dupes, it was a political statement. Every time that a political authority more or less exasperated by the social deterioration attempted to denounce the incompetent administration, they dispatched him a copy of his sex fantasies. If that didn't dissuade him, they liquidated him. Since I persisted so stubbornly, they arranged to keep me on my toes twenty-four hours a day…I was suspicious of everyone. Of my wife, my kids, the postman…and that is how I eventually landed up among the crazies.

We go out onto the veranda to watch the waves breaking on the reef. The waves are frisking about like whales. Their spray excites our lips. We avidly inhale the odor of the algae in order to void the foul air from our insides.

—Who's behind this…?

Dine puffs out his cheeks: The politico-financial mafia. That whoreson of a war is what provoked it, and what keeps it going. A collection of ex-politicians who cannot forgive having been removed from office—bosses of the old regime who grabbed everything they could lay their hands on, the kleptomaniacs—or those who've finished their down payments and have come back on the scene to exact revenge; sacked administrators, malcontents desiring to prove I know not what—an entire fraternity of irresponsible officials whose current charnel houses titillate the circling vultures.

—I want names, Dine, names…

—The name of the sect, growls Da Achour from the depths of his rocking chair. (He points to the sea in a trance.) Listen to the rolling waves, Llob. The waves are already panicking. The third millennium is awakening to the glory of the gurus…

Chapter nineteen

People don't like it when one blocks out their sun. It angers them and they react very badly. Salah Doba is aware of this. And that is why he has chosen to make himself very small. The little ones don't cast much of a shadow. They live camouflaged in their own. It protects them against misfortune. Salah Doba is smart. Being small doesn't stop one from thinking big, so it doesn't bother him. Furthermore, being small can be an advantage. The dwarfs are the last to get bricks on their heads and the first to spot when the tide rises. Consequently, what they lose in height they gain in perspective.

Administratively, Salah Doba is an underling in the basement of the Wafa National Bank, in the rue des Trois Pendules. In practice he is a multidisciplinary broker. His mission is to sort out distant markets for the benefit of the bigwigs of the old regime and to launder dirty money. He has the names of fictitious enterprises and phony transactions at his fingertips, and is reputed to be an ace in the field of false documents and their use. Thanks to his prowess, a large number of charismatic-and-so-forth persons have erected castles in Spain and enriched the Swiss banks. Contenting himself with the crumbs, like a good industrious and secretive ant, no one suspects what an empire he has managed to forge for himself behind his minuscule stature of insignificant civil servant.

His home resembles him. From the street, it is an ordinary looking building. Grotesque facade, unoriginal front door daubed a lurid orange, enough to make one despair of the constructor and go search for a wall to shore up. Then, all at once, having crossed the threshold, one lands in an oasis.

He receives us on the veranda. Humbly. As if his fortress was simply the fruit of our imagination. He's an emaciated fellow, with a metallic gaze and chronometrical gestures. He serves us lemonade, confectionaries from Paris and, moved to compassion by our appetite, he observes us smilingly in the manner of a charitable soul watching puppies eating.

—Monsieur Doba, Dine begins, licking his fingers, Superintendent Llob and I are reopening the Laouer affair.

—That's ancient history—

—I know. You were dismissed from your duties on account of your director's death. They tried to pin the responsibility for the holes they found in the coffers on you. But it was a matter of one hundred and twenty million dollars. A crater of that magnitude could only be the work of a gigantic excavator, and you are so frail…

Salah Doba's smile stretches still further as he propels the platter of candies in my direction as if it were a microphone.

—And what does Superintendent Llob think of this?

—I think that they used you.

He leans back in his chair, crossing his rodent fingers on his stomach.

—In that case we are in the same boat, Superintendent Llob. I got wind of your last exploit. You put an end to the schemes of Sid Lankabout. That's fine. Nonetheless, the fiesta continues.

—I don't see how we can be in the same boat, Monsieur Doba.

—They have used you as well.

—How is that?

He contemplates the sky. *A priori*, it isn't easy to impress him. Small as he is, he seems to rule his empire better than a shah. I find in him, once again, the attitude which Haj Garne, Sid Lankabout, and consort have displayed before my triviality.

—Superintendent, even from my position of a dismissed civil servant, I continue to command respect. The truth is that I have not been relieved of my functions, but only from indiscretions. That is the accepted procedure. As soon as a bead is drawn on a pawn he is placed on another square. As soon as things return to normal he is reintegrated in the setup.

—You are not answering my question.

He pouts in exasperation:

—Superintendent, generally, when one thinks oneself shrewd, one is nothing but the dupe.... Look, take the story of Abou Kalybse, what is it? It's quite simply the story of another shrewd fellow, another dupe. An emir who didn't figure on the official terrorist setup, and set out to make his own. Since what he was doing wasn't programmed, well, he undermined the existing choreography. Worst of all, the intruder did not balk at dipping into the financial reserves of the organization, and that was not at all good. He discredited the true financiers with their partners. It therefore became urgent to locate the cancerous cell. What was required was a good tracker, and who better than superintendent Llob? You bit the bait. Thanks to you we killed two birds with one stone. We got rid of the intruder, and did it legitimately. For the tax-paying public, the police have settled accounts with Sid Lankabout...alias Abou Kalybse. The affair is closed.

I try to discern a sardonic gleam in his pupils. Salah Doba is not joking.

—I am tired, Superintendent. Tired of stratagems, of manipulation, of complications. Go on home, it's friendly advice. You haven't got sufficient authority.

—We are stuntmen, says Dine.

—It's not worth the candle, gentlemen. Really, it's not worth the effort. Go on home.

Dine is not moved. He pecks away at the candies, his cheeks lumpy, he persists:

—It's not the one hundred and twenty million dollars that

bothers us, Monsieur Doba. The country is flat on its back. It would suit us to set it back on its feet.

Doba emits a hollow laugh:

—It's clear that you don't know what you are talking about.

—We are talking about the politico-financial mafia....

—Fantasies! Words, nothing but words, empty, fine-sounding phrases. Those people are the most powerful. Unassailable. They possess the rigor of the Crime Syndicate, the solidarity of the Casa Nostra, the immunity of parliamentarians and the impunity of the gods.

—One name, Monsieur Doba, just one single name. The rest, with all its risks, is up to us.

—What makes you think that I know one?

—We are in possession of documents, films, recordings. We know for example what it was that you went looking for in Beirut in '91, why you cut short your visit to Syria in '92, what happened to your two companions in the Libyan Desert in '94, why your mistress, de Staoueli, threw herself from the fifth story—

—That's enough. Since you have evidence, why don't you go ahead and arrest me? (In the face of our silence, he continues.) Wind! (He blows into the circle formed by his thumb and his index finger). Just wind! A wasted effort. You don't have the authority. Here it's neither Italy, nor France, nor the USA. Here justice prostitutes itself to the highest bidder. Basic values are tied to bank statements. If you have money you're great. Absolutely great. Really terrific. If you have no money, even if you are the Messiah, nobody gives a damn.

He consults his watch and says: It's time for my favorite soap opera. *Au revoir, Messieurs.*

We raise anchor.

Before taking our leave, I say to Salah Doba:

—The sole difference between you and the terrorists is that the terrorists take risks, and you do not. If their temerity does not minimize their cowardice, it renders you unworthy of contempt.

※

Of course we'd known, right from the outset, that Salah Doba was unshakable. There weren't too many illusions on that score. Our visit was simply a shot in the dark, on the off chance that it might yield something. You put out the word and you keep an ear out for the rumor. We had set up a listening post on the sixth story of a building, a hundred meters away from Salah's oasis. Our operator is literally spilling over his control panel, enormous and sweating, his earphones on his temples.

—Well? Dine inquires sitting down beside him.

The operator waves his pencil negatively. Twenty minutes later he stiffens, lifts his pencil to call for silence. The recorder's wheels whirr into motion with an irritating stridency.

—What's going on, a hoarse voice thunders at Salah Doba. It seems that you've received a visit from the cops.

—Two flies. Slightly irritating, but they don't bite.

—Have they been marked?

—Of no importance, I tell you. Small fry.

—What did they want?

—An old story. There is no fire, I assure you. If it were serious you can be sure I would have informed you.

—There had better not be any balls-ups, the other man shouts before hanging up.

I hear Salah Doba cursing his interlocutor…then silence! Dine, who had also been listening, inserts a finger into the hollow of his cheek.

—It's not good for him. What do we do?

—We wait.

The operator tears open a paper bag, extracts a gigantic sandwich from it and stuffs it into his mouth before I have the time to lick my lips in anticipation. I recommend that Dine get some rest. Hours pass. Slow, heavy, like a parade of pachyderms. I survey the street with binoculars. At times, at the whim of a visceral voyeurism, I light upon such and such a window, profaning people's intimacy. The operator dozes off. He snores, his feet on the control panel, his shirt open on a navel overflowing with sweat.

The sun begins its descent into hell. It plunges into the sea, attempts to gain the shore by grasping the waves, but the current of the open sea drags it down effortlessly, and it sinks in a spasm of rage and blood. Now stars are speckling the roof of the world. Night has already fallen on the city, with the moon like a punctured eye in the center of its forehead. In the distance the cars hazard their headlamps on the treacherous roads. The sirens scream panic-stricken behind the buildings. In an instant the streets are devitalized. Only the street lamps remain with the pavements in their consternating poverty.

Dine rejoins me.

Toward eleven PM a Mercedes appears at the end of the avenue, furtively drives along the street, overshoots Salah Doba's house, circles around, comes back, and stops in front of the orange door. A man gets out, rings the doorbell and steps back. Salah Doba appears in pajamas. We don't hear the explosions. The 'little one' falls down on the step, clutching his stomach. The killer bends over him, fires three bullets into his head.

—*Merde*! cries Dine.

I seize my transmitter and alert Lino and Bliss, who are waiting in ambush on the corner: Follow the Mercedes!

He hasn't gone far, the killer. He has parked his car in a garage, at the end of the neighborhood, and has disappeared inside a brothel. The piece of crap who is lounging at the reception desk waves us away with his hand before we have crossed the threshold.

—It's full.

I produce my badge with a magician's talent. He replies by tapping his register.

—My clients are in order. He ignores us and goes back to watching a televised boxing match.

—Would it bother you to attend to us?

—Sure, it would bother me a lot. I tell you that it's full up and that my clients are in order. If you wish to consult the register, it is there. I hate being disturbed when two lunatics are belting each other in the ring.

I stuff my arm through the grille, seize him by his Adam's apple and crush his face against the Plexiglas. His nose squashes against the glass, misting it up with steam. I have him gasping for air and suffocating.

—A comrade has just gone in. Black jacket and boots.

—Room 316, he gasps.

I propel him onto his TV and climb the stairs. Room 316 is at the start of the third story. We place ourselves on each side of the door, our guns at the ready. A woman's laughter rings out. The handle gives way under my hand. Through the half open door I see the comrade. He is in bed making a phone call, while a rounded and naked girl gently bites his shoulders.

—It was not foreseen, *habibo*, grumbles the comrade. I have a plane to catch tomorrow, before evening. I must have it, the money... it's not possible, *habibo*. I have delayed my departure three times.

The girl is the first to go rigid. With my finger I forbid her to sound the alarm. The *'habibo'* finally discovers us. His arm races for the gun on the chair.

—That would be idiotic, I dissuade him.

He hurls the phone at the wall, stretches himself full length on the bed, places his hands under his neck and grumbles:

—I told them that we should have liquidated you. They refused to listen to me. This is too dumb—letting myself be caught by an imbecile.

—Hey! What can you do? Not all people are the same.

Chapter twenty

Lino is engraving arabesques on the table with the point of his penknife. His unshod toes vitiate the rare gusts of air spared the stench from the bathroom. In the clammy silence of the office, only the rasping of the blade against the wood can be heard. Intermittently, the lieutenant blows on his calligraphy, greatly buoyed by his talent.

—I think I'll show it to the museum, afterward.

—Yes, along with your socks.

We are waiting for the phone call from Dine. Since I am on the wire-tapping panel, it appears, why not profit from it? Habibo is talking. He refused to speak without the presence of his lawyer and demanded he be handed over to the neighborhood commissariat. We took him to an isolated farm on the outskirts of the city, and we spent the night grilling him.

Habibo's name is Hamma Llyl. Employed in a bolt-making factory in Annaba, he had set it on fire the day after the extraordinary break-out of the nine hundred fundamentalists of Lambese. After several skirmishes in the underground, he specialized in urban terrorism. Eighteen assassinations in one year. His reputation has elevated him into the ranks of the most sought-after killers in the country. For the past two years he has been shuttling between Constantine and Algiers, a 9mm with a silencer in his toilet bag. He hunts only the big game: trade unionists, high officials, officers, editorial writers, troublesome emirs.

He doesn't know those who finance him. Even if he were permitted to approach them, he would decline the invitation, he says. A great many killers have been set off course on account of such a 'privilege'. The financiers pay well, but they are Medusas; anyone imprudent enough to lift his eyes to them, they turn to (tomb)stone.

Lino almost cuts himself with his blade when the phone rings. With a finger I beg him to be patient. At the sixth bleat he picks up: Central. Yes, go on, I'm listening.... Ah! It's you Superintendent Dine...I'm sorry, he's in a meeting. He gave me orders not to disturb him under any circumstances.... If you insist I shall go and see what I can do. Don't hang up.

He puts down the receiver, moves a chair, pretends to go out. I wait for three minutes, tap my feet on the ground, and then lift the receiver.

—Yes, Dine...? Listen, call me back in another hour. I'm up to my ears.

—It's extremely important.

—Have you found a fly in your glass?

—I've laid my hands on the fellow who was harassing you, the Habibo. He's a professional killer, Hamma Llyl, that's his name. He killed Salah Doba.

—Are you sure?

—Llob, do me a favor, postpone your bloody meeting. I tell you that this is a priority. The guy is pissing blood in the boot of my car. If you want to hear him with your own ears before he dies, get a move on.

—Bring him over here to me.

—Not a chance. There are too many spies. Meet me at Khelifa's in half an hour.

—Where exactly are you calling from?

—From a cabin about two kilometers from Sidi Moh.

I pretend to reflect:

—Not at Khelifa's. You know rue Gard...? No, listen; you remember the abandoned farm, in the vicinity of the salt lake, toward Douar Nayem?

—I know where you mean. Excellent idea. Let's meet there in an hour. One more thing, Llob. Come alone. I insist. Alone. One too many and the sky will fall on us.

༉

I am beginning to get a stiff neck from consulting my driving mirror. The city retreats behind the screen of the furnace. The motorway is feverish. I drive totally on the left, and I survey the cars which overtake and pass me in a devilish carousel.

Douar Nayem is as big as a pocket-handkerchief. Six decaying hovels, a crumbling patio and in the guise of a laundry room, a pool crawling with insects. The track leading to it has barely put in an appearance when it plays truant by disappearing. The fig trees rear their Christ heads the length of a hedge, hiding the misery of the slum. Not a shepherd to be seen. The village is deserted. The villagers have fled the violent exigencies of the armed bands.

The farm is about a hundred meters behind undergrowth comprised of cricket calls and evil looking bushes; an ideal spot for traps. Dine is waiting for me in the yard, equipped with a bulletproof vest and a small bore pistol. He points to a vest: Wrap up well if you don't wish to catch cold.

A blackbird soliloquizes in the copse. An indolent breeze teases the wild grass. The countryside lets itself be overcome by the heat wave; it's reminiscent of camping under canvas.

—Here they come! Dine alerts me, banging the chamber of his weapon.

A small truck leaves the road, climbs toward the hamlet, circles the pool, then the copse and comes to a halt about fifty meters away. Its doors open on a group of five armed and hooded individuals, wearing gaudy attire. Chater's men, in ambush nearby, don't give them time to deploy.

A strong burst of fire mows down two of the terrorists. The

other three, taken unawares, attempt to regain the copse. The bursts of fire sweep over them and they collapse. The truck reverses, overturns on the body of a wounded man, and uproots a bush. It is immediately caught in a hail of fire. Its reserve tank ignites, setting the rest of the bodywork on fire. A human torch ejects itself screaming, whirls around and goes on to burn itself out on a rocky mound.

It has all happened very quickly, as in a dream. The silence that follows plunges the hill into a parallel world. Already Lieutenant Chater and his men are springing from their trench, at the ready, and advancing toward the scene of butchery. Stretched out on a tuft of grass, a huge creature breathes its last, its chest shredded. Its bloodied hand fails to reach the Kalachnikov lying on the ground nearby. Dine kicks away the weapon, bends over the wounded man, and tears off his hood: it's Ghoul Malek's albino.

Chapter twenty-one

I gaze at Algiers and Algiers gazes at the sea. This city has no more emotions. There is only disenchantment as far as the eye can see. Its symbols are discarded. Subjected to an obligatory silence, its history bends its spine and its monuments belittle themselves.

Algiers is currently reliving its obsessions. Its troubadours no longer sing. Wherever their muse takes them, they see it muzzled. Their hands, orphaned twice, not once—firstly from the flute which is stopped up, then from the pen which is assassinated—can no longer feel the pulse of the land as they once did when we were sorcerers and water-diviners.

Algiers is a malaise; the dream is punctured there like an abscess.

Algiers is a place where many die. There, God has the function of a sedative; no one wants to believe that happiness is a question of one's state of mind any more. Algiers is an itinerant drama: its tomorrows will have no more respect for an irresolute specter than have jackals for one of their pack who has weakened.

I park my Zastava at the top of Notre Dame. In the distance, beyond the port bristling with sad-looking cranes, the *Maqam* stands forgotten on his hill, resembling a huge, retarded boy. I see the *Casbah* crucified in perjury, like the remains of a grasshopper savaged by ants. Times have changed.

It wasn't altogether unhappy once upon a time, the *Casbah*. It had immense faith. It was proud of its craftsmen, of its shoemakers, and of the fezzes worn by its shopkeepers. Above all, it knew how to share its joys and to keep its troubles to itself. There was Dhamane the tattooist who executed stunning frescoes on the chests of pimps and on the arms of sailors. There was Roukaya la Guerisseuse, a blind centenarian, whose furtive fingers knitted together the severest fractures with the merest touch. There was Alilou Domino who would beat his interminable rivals in double quick time; that very same Alilou who died from apoplexy the day when, distracted by the drunkenness of Moha Didou, he forgot to rid himself of his double six. There was the doe-eyed Bahja la Vestale whom nobody dared approach for fear of seeing her vanish like a *houri*...

We were all poor, but like the water-lilies that the stagnant waters of the pond did not affect, we floated on the surface of harsh disappointments with a rare sobriety, keeping watch for the slightest light to be inspired by it.

Then, upon the hatching of the cocoon and before the *auto-da-fe* of oaths, our memories became 'deprived of sun'; evening settled in our hearts; a moonless and starless evening, without daring or tender passion, a half-light hung like a spider's web in which our prayers have grown faint.

⁂

I went to the office to collect hundreds of photos of victims of terrorism. Lino asked me whether it was for my next book. I didn't answer him. I went over to 13 rue des Pyramides. Ghoul Malek wasn't home. I broke a window and let myself into the palace. I spent two hours pinning the photos on the walls, the pictures, the knick-knacks, the carpets, the curtains, the chairs. Unbearable photos depicting children with their throats slit, raped women, decapitated elders, exhumed mothers, dismembered soldiers, poor illustrious tortured individuals. Once my decor was spread out over the indecent opulence of the furnishings, I stretched myself full length on a sofa and stared at the ceiling hard enough to split it. Night fell like a mask. I didn't put on any lights. I continued smoking.

A car gargles in the courtyard, then silence. Steps ring out on the stairs. A clicking of keys and the door gives way before the elephantine stature of Ghoul Malek.

—Cherif! he calls out.

The chandelier lights up.

—What's this, this mess! cries the incredulous *nabob*.

—It's your masterpiece, Monsieur Ghoul.

For a full five seconds he remains speechless on discovering me behind him.

—Who let you enter here? Where is Cherif?

—If you mean your Moby Dick, he has sunk for good.

His face is on fire, his jowls vibrate: How did you dare to come over here?

—I am still wondering about that.

—Are you out of your mind, Superintendent?

—Let us say that I've lost many friends.

It's a pleasure to see his Adam's apple bouncing about in his crimson throat. He recovers immediately and makes for the phone.

—Not worth it, Monsieur Ghoul. We are completely cut off from the rest of the country. There are only the four of us: the Devil, God, you and me.

—You are ridiculous, Superintendent. Collect this entire circus and get out! I've had a rough day. I need to be alone. He walks off.

—Ghoul!

My shout stops him in his tracks.

—I know everything.

He nods his head, comes back, leans against an armchair and eyes me with contempt: What you don't know, Superintendent, is what a pit you are digging yourself. Miserable little creatures of your kind don't stand up against me, they are exposed…. You came to arrest me? You cannot even believe it yourself. One does not arrest Ghoul Malek…. What did you hope to achieve with your idiotic picture exhibit? Touch my conscience? Arouse my compassion? Make me feel guilty? Imbecile. If so, you have not understood anything. Ever since the world has existed, society has obeyed a threefold dynamic of those with the upper hand: those who govern, those who crush, and those who supervise. A *rais** doesn't require gray matter, his crown is quite sufficient. You Superintendent, your *kepi** suits you perfectly. Be content to keep your blinkers on straight. The rest doesn't concern you. There exists, within the social hierarchy, a motorizing force. It is not noticed by governments or their subjects. The notion of scruples means nothing to it. It has no need to worry about what is forbidden. The only thing that motivates it is how to boot the nation's behind so that it doesn't fall asleep on its dung heap.

I cannot explain what suddenly comes over me. The fury that helped me to overcome the agony of the waiting, earlier on, the thoughts and words that mobilized me on the sofa vanish, flee from me, creating a void around me. I have to admit that the swine intimidates me. His glance diminishes me, makes me retreat underground. It seems to me that if he were to raise his hand I would take to my heels without looking back. This abominable human being, this monster has turned us into objects for thirty years. I can hardly believe that I manage to remain standing before him. And he goes on talking, talking.... In my bubbling head, fragments flare, come and go.

—Every country has need of a crisis to recycle itself, he continues. Naturally there is some damage. But what is a handful of martyrs compared with a renaissance? It's actually a necessity. It makes one believe in the motherland and it prepares one for the sacrifices of tomorrow. The only areas where people have any say are the vote and war. You are an idealist, Monsieur Llob; you have a Utopian idea of patriotism. However you yourself are ridiculously obsolete. The world transforms itself at the whim of its appetites. From now onward nationalism is only to be evaluated as a function of interests. They are its guarantee, its survival. Today our country is being bled white so it can be delivered of a new Algeria by cesarean section—a country of tomorrow, modern, strong, ambitious. We got off to a bad start in 1954. Our revolution proved a fiasco—and the proof, after thirty years of independence, is in its regression, totalitarianism, and the rule of the mediocre. This war is not a malediction. It's a godsend, an amazing chance, sheer Providence. We are taking charge of it. We control it. It's our password, the duty we have to pay so as not to be excluded from the new world order. To progress from a caricature of a socialist system to the opening up of the market, we must pay the customs duty. That's what we are doing at the moment. We are going to rebuild a country capable of negotiating its potential without having to humble itself.

He shows me the door, orders me to leave and walks away.

—I hate to shoot people in the back, I warn him.

His hand on the banister, he turns to face me, gazes at my gun contemptuously and lets out a Homeric laugh.

—You must be completely out of your mind, Superintendent.

I hear myself stammering:

—There are three instances when men are judged—by conscience, justice and God. It happens that the first two fail now and again, but not the third. And that is the option that awaits you now.

His features fade all of a sudden. He becomes livid; his lips are drained.

—You can't be serious, Superintendent. You're just a cop. You don't have the right.

—I fear that it is the only right remaining to me.

When I recover my composure, I am surprised to find myself pressing on the trigger like a lunatic, long after the barrel of my gun has cooled.

Glossary

Abou Kalybse—Algerian play on words based on the French word 'apocalypse'. "Abou" (father of) and "kalybse," which can be read "kalypse" since the letter P doesn't exist in the Arabic alphabet.

Bliss—the devil, whom in Koranic tradition, the woman is said to resemble. In 1990 the FIS (Islamic Salvation Front) slogan for the municipal elections was "*Dad Bliss, Vote FIS*" (Against the Devil, vote FIS).

Casbah—the older section of a city in northern Africa or the Middle East.

Dine—religion; also the beginning of the Arabic insult "*Naa dine babek*" or "Cursed be the religion of your father."

Fatiha—opening sura of the Holy Koran, that doubles as the creed of Islam and as a salutation that expresses strong feelings and important events in life, such as love, births, marriages and burials.

Fatwa—Moslem religious ruling

Ghoul—the ogre, the wicked landlord

Habibo—friend

Haj Garne—the horn

Houri—one of the beautiful virgins of the Koranic paradise

Imam—religious leader, also the prayer leader in a mosque

Kepi—French military hat with a flat circular top and a visor

Lankabout—spider

Maqam—'Maqam Es Chahid'—Monument of the Martyrs

Mederassas—Moslem religious seminaries where the Koran is studied.

Mullah—male religious leader or teacher

Minbar—the pulpit in a mosque

Nabob—rich, wealthy man

Nahs—misfortune

Nota bene—(n.b.) used to direct attention to something particularly important.

October 1988—In October 1988 serious demonstrations that broke out across Algeria to protest against commodity shortages and high prices were broken up by police and army troops supported by armored vehicles. More than five hundred people were killed after badly trained soldiers used automatic weapons against the demonstrators.

Rais—president or leader

Ramadan—the ninth month of the year in the Islamic calendar, during which Moslems fast from sunrise to sunset.

Shabban—the eighth month of the year in the Islamic calendar

Sunna—the tradition of the Koran

Taghout—"one who exceeds his legitimate limits"; dictator. Word used by the Islamists to designate government employees down to the simple policemen.

Tahar Djaout—a novelist, poet and journalist who was attacked by fundamentalist assassins as he was leaving his home in Bainem in May 1993. He died in June after lying in a coma for a week.

About the Author

Yasmina Khadra

Yasmina Khadra is the pen name of Mohammed Moulessehoul, an Algerian army officer born in 1956, who adopted a woman's pseudonym to avoid military censorship. Moulessehoul held a high rank in the Algerian army, and despite the publication of several successful novels in Algeria, only revealed his true identity in 2001, after going into exile and seclusion in France. He is uniquely placed to comment on vital issues of the Middle East, Algeria and fundamentalism. *Newsweek* acclaims him as "one of the rare writers capable of giving a meaning to the violence in Algeria today."

Khadra's previous books, *In the Name of God* and *Wolf Dreams*, have also been published by *The* Toby Press.

The fonts used in this book are from the Garamond family

Other works by Yasmina Khadra
published by *The* Toby Press

In the Name of God

Wolf Dreams

The Toby Press publishes fine writing,
available at bookstores everywhere. For more information,
please contact *The* Toby Press at www.tobypress.com